HERE BE ICEBERGS

First published by Charco Press 2022
Charco Press Ltd., Office 59, 44-46 Morningside Road,
Edinburgh, EH10 4BF

First published in Spanish as *Aquí hay icebergs*
by Penguin Random House Grupo Editorial S.A. (Peru)

A CIP catalogue record for this book is available from the British Library.

ISBN: 9781913867195
e-book: 9781913867201

www.charcopress.com

Edited by Robin Myers
Cover designed by Pablo Font
Typeset by Laura Jones
Proofread by Fiona Mackintosh

Printed by TJ Books Limited

Katya Adaui

HERE BE ICEBERGS

Translated by
Rosalind Harvey

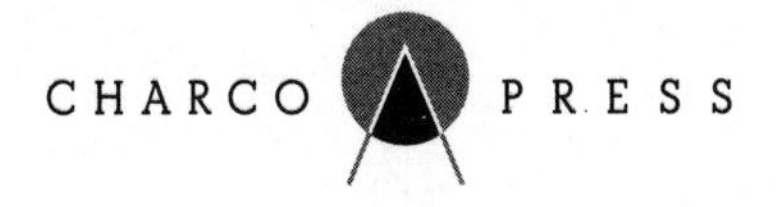

CONTENTS

1.

THE HUNGER ANGEL

68.

My mother brings me offerings on Sundays. The past returns in occurrences. She insists on furnishing me with new memories. Her own.

A month ago: Look what I've got for you. From a bag she removes a pair of little baby shoes. They look like they've been dipped in copper. Living fossils, seahorses. They were yours, you wore them in your first month. There are photos of you with them on – don't you like them? My face, frozen in horror. Why don't you take those books off the table and display them?

Last Sunday: I found your stamp album, it wasn't stolen after all. You used to love the Magyar Posta stamps so much! And that time you gave us a talk on Australia in the living room and showed us all the kangaroo stamps.

It's true: I love philately just as I love literature. Both show a version of reality, selective acts, counterfeits.

This Sunday: This might surprise you! She hands me a piece of paper.

Growth Chart and Record of Immunisations. My surname has a superfluous 'G'. The handwriting is not either of my parents'.

Birth. Length: 19 inches. Weight: 7 pounds 14 ounces.

The last recorded date: 5 years old. 3 foot 11 inches. Weight: 3 stone 4.

The last four annual inoculations: Polio. MMR. Polio. Polio.

All hand-written, month after month. In my mother's painstaking cursive. At the bottom of the page:

SQUIBB – Products Made Specially for Children
Confidence that Comes from a Century of Experience

I interpret these peculiar objects parachuting down onto me: you exist because of me. I cared for you. I loved you. Now it's your turn: love me, care for me. I exist.

67.

I went to clean the maid's room and guess what I found? All your maths exercise books. They're the only ones you didn't throw away.

66.

I miss your father. Don't you?

I miss him in a quiet sort of way.

So you didn't love him, then.

65.

Mum is good. I don't know any longer if she is cruel or mad, but she is good. She gave us the best school, she gave us holidays.

You repeat everything she says, even today.

You just don't get it. She's old, she's on her own.

She's exactly how she wanted to be.

What happened to Dad was a shock for her, the poor thing. We'll have to take it in turns to go and visit her. I can't spend all my Saturdays looking after her. I want to see my husband, too. And I have to work. I'm going to Recife next month, to a conference on leishmaniasis.

Well, don't do anything out of guilt.

It's not guilt. It's pity.

Your pity looks a lot like your guilt.

Yeah, maybe; perhaps it is guilt.

When we say goodbye, my sister never quite manages to say: You're going? She says: You're abandoning me?

The mark is the mark.

64.

My aunt: Your father confessed to me years ago that he once thought about committing suicide in his car. He stopped because he glanced up at the rear-view mirror and saw you sitting in the back seat.

63.

My brother doesn't work. I tell everyone he works. And what does he do? Oh, all kinds of things. Please don't let anyone ask me how long it's been since I last saw him, how long he's been away for, whether he's happy doing what he does. I don't even know where he is right now. I could make up an entire backstory for him. I've even forgotten his voice; he did have one, clear as a covenant. How do I fit him into my life? I don't know.

62.

I never hit you, darling, it was your brother.

He never hit me, but it's in the past now, Dad. I've forgiven you.

What have you forgiven me for if I didn't do anything to you?

Forget it, it's in the past.

Just the same, forgive me anyway.

I brush his hair with my fingers. I smile. Kiss his forehead. Draw the curtains that separate us from the others. What you do think you have?

I'm not an idiot.

Come on, Dad, let's talk. Tell me something.

Where's your sister?

At the billing department, paying.

Oh, of course. Yep, spend away, you'll get it all back from the insurance anyway, as you know.

Don't worry about that. Do you want Mum to come and visit? Would you like to see her?

No, I don't want her to see me like this, sick as a dog. I want to see my son. It's been such a long time now.

61.

Don't forget to cut my nails, she says, every Sunday. I cut Mum's nails. They ping off in all directions. I don't do this for anybody. Cutting nails disgusts me, like squeezing spots, whiteheads, like holding my head over the toilet bowl to puke. I balance her feet on my knees; she's entrusting me with her comfort, not her beauty. She's chosen me as her pedicurist. Our nails look alike, as all nails do, but they are ours: hers, hard; mine, a little softer. It must be because of the extra calcium – she never goes anywhere without her pillbox. I keep a few of the nails when she's not looking, just as she still has a lock of my baby hair, a different colour to what it is now.

60.

You can't marry him.

I love him.

No you don't, you just want to get laid.

That's not true.

You liar, you should be ashamed of yourself. What you don't realise is that men only ever see you as a hole. Don't get married. I'd rather you just shacked up with the man.

I move out the next day. I take my bedside table, a mattress. A box with all the letters and postcards I've ever received. My CDs. My books. Tickets from gigs and museums. My notebooks. So little life even in my collections, but this is what I am.

You'll soon come crawling back with your tail between your legs, just you wait!

She shouts at me in the street while I help the driver to load my things faster into the van. You're a whore, that's what you are.

My sister. Where's my sister? Where is she crying over us?

The book whose title names me: The Hunger Angel.

59.

Why are you calling her, Maurito? She's a bad, bad girl. My daughter's no good for you. You've no idea what she does to me. When are you coming round? I'll give you a prayer card. You're the only friend of hers I can stand because you're a Catholic from a good family, like me. You and I are the same, you know. *You* love your mother, I'm sure of it.

58.

How could I not love your brother? He's my child too, isn't he? The problem is your father never loved him. They used to compete for my love.

57.
I ring your house and your mother tells me not to trust you because you're bad. What is it with your old lady?

56.
Valeria comes back every summer. She keeps her promises. We recommend books to each other. Once – without knowing it – it turned out we'd been reading the same book at the same time. She writes to me:

Nena, I dreamed about you and now it feels like we were together just a little while ago. In the dream I was happy you were there, and at the same time I felt sad because you were about to leave. But you were close by and it was so lovely.

Our friendship values memory, shares a weight. We measure everything in relation to our day-to-day life: her house, my house. The families we would eventually cease to belong to. She wants to be an actress. I, a writer. When they see us chatting at the edge of the pool, the adults: Don't they look lovely, always so relaxed.

They're wrong. We're practising how to endure everything life has in store for us.

55.
I get home from school. Mum is in bed. Anaesthetised eyes on high alert.

What was the operation for this time?

How do you know? Who told you?

She smells of formaldehyde.

I'll show you – undo my blouse.

A long scar on her belly, the stitches thick, fresh. They sliced off her nipples, took out fat, sewed them back on. Or something like that. A DIY project. An autopsy.

My friend Jonathan did it for free. Don't say a word to your sister or I'll kill you.

Why did you have surgery? You had a nice body.

You said it: *had*, a long time ago. When you're my age you'll understand. It's a tragedy to feel young, see yourself in the mirror, and realise you're not.

When my mother goes to parents' evenings, everyone stares at her. She is tall and blonde, her permed hair cropped short. She smokes like she's in an advert, she is a red mouth producing clouds that seem to cocoon her, to do her good. Her chic skirts are paired with handbags and jewellery, everything matching: not so much dressed as linked together like a chain. I brim with pride. This woman is my mother and she is absolutely beautiful. Men shout at her in the street. She smiles at each and every tribute. Success is all your friends wanting to be adopted by your mother. At home, I find my mother's ugliness offensive.

One day she comes back from work with a blue outline tattooed onto her eyelids, little dots of blood like red crusts of sleep. Her lips are surrounded by the raised rough skin of micro wounds.

What have you done to yourself?

They asked me to be a model at the hairdressers. The permanent eye- and lip-liner was free. I get everything for free. You know that everyone loves me.

Before going to sleep, she places her upper set of dentures on the bedside table. She lost most of her teeth in a car accident at the age of eighteen. The dentist decided to take them all out, to create a black hole.

What can I say, darling? That's what they did back then.

I don't understand this fashion. Like my aunt who draws on her eyebrows; she plucked the hairs of her real ones one by one one by one one by one, until she killed them off completely. The colour of Mum's false teeth looks natural. Even though she smokes. In a late-night Italian film, a woman removes her upper set of dentures; now the protagonist can kiss her more deeply. They enjoy it. Mum never kisses anyone, not even Dad when he comes to visit her. She gets everything for free. It embarrasses me to think this about Mum.

Did Dad know you wore dentures?

Yes, he always knew. Well, he's got a few false teeth of his own. He sticks them in himself with Moldimix.

So he loved you just the way you were.

Your father is incapable of loving anyone.

She won't let us see her without her dentures in. Walking to her room, I press into the floor with my socks; I know where it creaks, where it's out of tune; I look at her wrinkled mouth, puckered as if she's just sucked on some acidic fruit, then at her set of teeth (a stuffed creature's dentures); I wonder if Mum's voice changes when it's toothless. Does it become the voice of an old woman? The thought of this terrifies me. Would I recognise her?

A question for her former dentist: Why did you fast forward my mother's old age?

You know why I'm so hard on you, don't you? Mum has a question for me, along with the answer: So that you'll be the strongest of all my children.

54.

Dad moans about his teeth. He can't chew meat anymore. He swallows great big pieces, he chokes. He's pulled out the wastepipe, I say, gently teasing, of his gullet plumbing. He laughs. For the first time he agrees to seek medical help. The dentist orders a set of lower dentures to be made for him. He can't understand how my father has got by this whole time with teeth he glues in himself.

Did he stick them straight on to the gum? Or somewhere else? we wonder.

Dad's madness: returning to the soup-and-puree phase.

The first thing he does with his new teeth is smile at us for no reason to speak of. His cheeks are a little less slack now. His smile is younger than he is. He doesn't thank me. He is thankful.

53.
Do you know how deep the roots of these trees are? my sister asks. I shoot her a filthy look. We're in Dad's car, all three of us. Her and her outbursts.

52.
You and your brother both smeared shit all over your cot. Your sister, not once. She was always a much cleaner little thing.

51.
Mum kicks Dad out. She changes the entire lock mechanism, the bolts, the chain. Dad steps back from the door and looks up at the house, wondering why something he's been able to access for the last twenty years is now rejecting him. He moves into an apartment in a strange neighbourhood. Don't come and visit, he tells me and my sister. I ask him to come on a trip with me. It's the first time I'm allowed to invite someone. I promise him the jungle. He says he won't come. I call on him one evening – it's the final of the Copa Sudamericana. I have a couple of beers in my backpack. It takes Dad a moment to recognise my voice. He lets me in. Turns his back to me. I address his back. He turns around. Cuts and bruises on his face.

They tied me to a chair, put my alpaca jumper in my mouth, I couldn't breathe. I was there for hours, trying to free myself.

And what were you thinking, Dad?

I was thinking: Don't kill me, because my daughter's about to take me on a trip.

We drink our beers.

We've never travelled as a family before, not even the two of us alone. Seven hours on a bus. By a waterfall, a shaman gives us a putrid-smelling good luck charm stuffed with rotting seeds. We cross a rope bridge suspended over a tangled forest that spreads further than the eye can see. We love this brutality. Like our own, it does not ask for permission. We dress up like indigenous people in a village where the inhabitants hide their satellite dish as soon as we show up. We are chased by a monkey that fails to catch us; it's tied to a tree with a long rope. We eat the fish we pull from the river. We'll return to the city in a feral state, we'll be smoked meat, cacao, barefoot river, biological fluctuations, colonisation.

In the bus on the way back we promise each other: Now we're going to live, that's how things are.

I try my luck.

I ask Dad what happens when someone drinks bleach:

It's better to commit suicide with rat poison, it turns your blood to water. The strongest brand is called Champion. When my son died, I thought about killing myself. If I had, I wouldn't have had you girls. Don't kill yourself. We come into this world with pain and we'll leave it painfully when it's our time. I read this somewhere, and I say it over and over to myself: 'We would all love to live forever, but how terrible it would be to never die.'

I give him one of my headphones to share my songs with him; I use the other one to listen. We want to believe it. To live is a decision. We won't be born again. To live is to stand up for ourselves.

50.
One night, Dad and I sleep in his car, outside our house. Mum bolts the door.

I pay for this house and you'll inherit it someday, Dad says; who is she to take away my rights?

My mother lets me in. It's OK, he won't come in, I promise. Just me.

I betrayed my father in exchange for a house, a house that stopped inhabiting me as soon as I agreed to the swap. He will no longer live here. He will return, like a guest forever on probation.

49.
You're the spitting image of your father. Your sister's the one who looks most like me.

48.
Prepared to do anything, Mum says to Dad: How can you love someone if your mother was bed-ridden when she had you? (And in a whisper: If your father practically raped her?). How can you love someone if you watched your own son die?

Dad parries: Don't you bring my mother into this. How dare you bring my son into this, for god's sake?

They hit each other. I step between them. He picks me up off the floor and she slaps at me in the air. They are giants united by one identical moment: lethal – match and touchpaper. It's crystal clear to me: I am not what unites them.

I ask myself: How will I ever be able to love?

How can I start to fix things if everything is broken?

Who loves what's broken?

I am not them. I write and I save myself. It happens to me, but I manage to be The Spectator.

47.
Dad doesn't move from his room. Lying sick in bed, nothing wrong with him, everything wrong. Come in. Smell of cigarettes, scent of perfume. I stand in the doorway, I ask him: Tell me you love me.

I use actions to show my affection.

Tell me you love me.

Clear off.

Dad.

No.

He gets out of bed. With both hands, he pushes at the door to close it. No. No and no. We struggle. He shuts the door on my foot.

46.
Mum says the rosary every Thursday. She worships a fat little Buddha. It was a gift from a Colombian sculptor. She says: I sat him on my lap on the plane so nothing would happen to him.

She plays the lottery, puts the tickets at the base of the little figure, turns on the light in his hollow plaster belly, rubs him several times a week, a miracle's a miracle, it doesn't matter who performs it. She talks to him.

Mum talks to her plants and to her Buddha. To her plants to make them grow, and to the Buddha for every occasion. The Buddha knows all her desires.

When my brother comes back from his first trip, he lifts the Buddha up over his head. He holds it up high, hammering at the air. Mum watches him, mutely. *Just one word from you would be enough to save me.* The Buddha falls. It smashes, impossible to salvage.

My brother: Now you know how it feels to have someone take away the thing you love the most.

He goes away again. When he comes back, he stays in hotels. He has lost his room at our house. His room is Dad's room now. Mum puts down a rug where the smashed Buddha left a dent in the wooden floorboards. She replaces it with a Chinese dragon. It has a cracked foot glued back on with Moldimix. After polishing the living room floor, she never forgets to pull the rug back over the dent.

45.

Dad asks me: How about you cooperate and change the lightbulb in the living room. You've got long fingers.

I hate this police-like 'cooperate', as if I never '*cooperated*'. He forgets to turn off the electricity. I am hurled onto the sofa. I land in a seated position, as if I'd been like that the whole time, talking to him about the living room lightbulb. We laugh.

44.

It's Christmas again. On the radio, Roberto Carlos is singing about wanting to have a million friends.

Mum: Let's give thanks to the Lord that we're a family.

I say: That we're really good at pretending to be a family.

She says: You're so mean all the time. I don't know where you get it from!

My sister: Come on, don't fight.

Dad: Aren't they going to play some Christmas carols?

Me: You know in the carol 'The Fishes in the River', how can the Virgin 'brush her hair in between the curtains'?

Mum: Seriously? You're going to ruin Christmas again? Well, are you?

Dad: There you go – a leg for you and the other one for me.

Me: And for this turkeycide, amen.

The plates that spend the whole year displayed in

the dining room cabinet are brought out cyclically for the Christmas ritual. In the midst of all the magnificent decorations, a plastic jug with the logo of a brand of matches spoils the fantasy. I detest it.

Just like every year, my parents give each other forty packs of cigarettes, the same brand.

The next day for breakfast, we eat the things that survived us unharmed. The remains of the turkey.

43.

Four in the morning.

Mum is vacuuming her dresser drawers, again. She lifts out each empty drawer, drops it onto the floor. I can't sleep. I go into her room, I'm going to shout, I'm going to drill into her night, too. She disarms me: Why are you out of bed, sweetie? You'll wake your sister, go back to bed.

42.

It's you girls' fault I can't leave your father.

41.

On the last curve, I give it my all. I waste my second wind. It's the 4×400 metres relay. Before I reach the finish line in second place, I faint. The cardiologist gives me a stress test. He finds a murmur. When he puts the sticky patches on my back: Your scoliosis is really bad.

I stop running.

40.

On the day of my birthday I meet Valeria for the first time in the club's swimming pool. Her friendship is like swimming, like feeling in motion. Despite our own sisters, we choose each other with no sense of betrayal. I can tell her what my life is like, listen to hers, and feel that we're the same without needing to be totally alike.

We smile at each other from our towels. Valeria lives in Buenos Aires. She promises: I'll come back next summer.

39.
I listen to Mum tell a friend on the phone: I would eat shit for my children.

38.
When your sister was in fourth grade, she was once asked to paint Jesus for her homework, Mum tells me. We bought her card and felt-tip pens. Every afternoon, when she got home from school, she would draw. She said she would do it all in pencil first, then felt-tip pen, and finally colour it all in. I think she must have used up a whole rubber, because I spent all my time sweeping up what she rubbed out. It took her a week to finish it. Your dad said: Let's see how the little one does when she gets the same task next year – then we'll know how different they are. And what do you think happened the following year? You called us after half an hour: I've finished! Your dad said: No, not like that, you have to take things seriously, your Jesus isn't even crucified. That's how I see him, you replied, and went outside to play. It was then that we knew: Your sister would have a much harder time.

37.
After going for a run, once I've had lunch, I read on my bed. I read a book a day. I read everything. I have several families. If you're going to read a book in my class you can leave the classroom, my maths teacher tells me; you're so different to your sister! Just as some of my friends smoke in secret, I read anywhere I can. At all hours. If I'm playing French skipping, I get told when it's my turn; I read standing up, the rope creeping up towards my ankles, my knees, my armpits. I am given a diploma signed by

two nuns: For being an outstanding reader.

Get your nose out of that book! Mum keeps her books under lock and key. She tells me I'll be old enough soon, that they're a little grown up for me now. She is obsessed with using ornamental jars as hiding places. I find the key, every single time. In Mum's books the characters have sex. Dad mostly reads Agatha Christie, and almost always guesses who the murderer is; they all have a motive to kill the dead person.

I read; it's the same as running away. I find a spot. My bed. The treehouse. Eighty days around the world. A room of one's own. And if I don't understand what I read (this happens a lot), I seethe.

36.
Me and Mariano have a pizza eating contest. Him: thirteen slices. Me: ten. We ring all the buzzers on the block and, when someone answers, we burp into the intercom. We kiss each other in my parents' garage, I press up close to him, stick my tongue in his mouth, he rubs himself up against me, my first orgasm.

35.
Mum holds up my Discman: You love this, don't you? She pretends to drop it, pretends to change her mind.

34.
I run the hundred metres on the new Tartan track. Someone has lent me a pair of men's running shoes with spikes. They're too big for me. I reach the finish line at the same time as Paloma, my right shoe beating hers. In the photo Paloma is beating me. You look like a gazelle, the athletics teacher tells me. You're a born runner. On Fridays, after class, she makes me run 3,000 metres. My time is twenty-five minutes.

33.
It's you girls' fault I can't leave your mother. For better or worse, she's the mother of my children.

32.
We still wash ourselves with a bucket and a little jug. If she's annoyed, Mum chases me with the bucket of hot water. She fires up fast like the new immersion heater. I'm getting faster all the time. I shut myself in mine and my sister's room. The lock is broken. I can't hold the door shut for long. She forces her way in, I jump from bed to bed, I reach the door. I escape. She never catches me. I promise myself that one day I will write the story of an athlete who wins all his races by imagining he's being chased. I don't tell anyone, but I find it hard to wash myself, to see myself naked. Outside the upstairs bathroom is the only full-length mirror in the house. I follow my body with a compact mirror. I open and close my legs. I look at my back, what does it look like?

31.
The terrorists blow up the electricity pylons. The constant power cuts make it difficult to read, to do chores. Living under the threat of bombs is a hunt; only a few adults deal with it sympathetically. No one comprehends it – horror cannot be understood. Our parents take us to see the craters made by the bombs. I don't know what they expect of us girls. The city pains me, not the country. Not yet. We are under curfew. Candle factories are the only places that seem to be doing all right. The candles are slender and white, like the ones lit during peace ceremonies. The food goes off in the fridge. One morning for breakfast, my sister and I share a tamal from the day before (from the day before the power failed). We both end up in the toilets at school. Our stomachs are a mess. Each of us in a

single bed in the infirmary. The nurse makes us oregano tea. We giggle in between the spasms, the cold sweats. Mum asks her boss for permission to go and pick us up: My daughters never get ill at the same time.

30.

I don't feel able to sit my maths exam. I wake up in the middle of the night. My stomach hurts from the nerves. I soak cotton balls, throw them down the toilet, one after another. Have you got diarrhoea, sweetheart? I manage to wake Mum up. I manage to trick her. I don't go to school the next day. She lets me stay in her room. I've got this whole bed to myself, no one can see me, I roll around. I watch TV for hours, kids' cartoons. She brings me chicken soup, seasoned with oregano and a lump of melting parmesan. She comes upstairs regularly to check if I need anything. What would you like most of all? she asks. She kisses me all over my face, confirming: You don't have a fever. There's no infection, you'll feel better soon.

Being ill feels a lot like happiness.

29.

Grandma: I would give more for one of your sister's legs than for all of you.

A week later she's in the clinic in a coma. Seven days in silence. I love her. I did steal her stamps, it's true, but I pretend not to notice when she gives me back the Christmas presents I'd given her wrapped in different paper. They let me have some time alone with her. I hold her hand and speak to her. Nobody at home knows I'm awake at five in the morning listening to their phone conversations. No one tells me the truth. At school I have to read out Bible passages to the whole class. As I read, I cry. My grandma is dead. They send me home:

the first loss. I don't want to go up to the coffin. They make me. Why does she have cotton wool in her nose and ears?

It's not to stop dust from getting in, it's to stop anything from coming out.

I regret not having asked her more questions about the two World Wars. If I had said to her: The First World War wasn't a world war, it was a European one – how would she have reacted?

28.
Dad and I wake up early because we're thirsty. He goes downstairs to the kitchen. His flip-flop footsteps sound like they're applauding him as they flap against the floor. He comes back upstairs with plastic cups filled with boiled water. His is red. Mine is blue. We each have our own brightly coloured plastic cup.

27.
Draw the thing that most stood out for you over the holidays, the teacher tells us. I draw a TV and on the screen I write: Ten Dead in Terrorist Attack.

The teacher calls my mother to arrange a meeting with her.

Mum tells her: But she doesn't watch the news. She doesn't even watch TV.

Ah, says the teacher, your daughter is aware that she is aware.

26.
Auntie, guess which is my side of the room!

This one.

How can you tell?

There are no crosses.

25.
Mum: If you carry on doing badly at school, you'll amount to one of two things: a prostitute, or a drug addict.

24.
We're on our way back from school in Dad's car. We want chocolate. My sister crosses the road without looking both ways. Dad calls to her from the car. He covers his eyes. He can't bear to look, because if he does… A car has just missed my sister. She walks over to us with her hands full. For the whole drive home, Dad doesn't say a word. My sister and I chat away to each other. We get our fingers all sticky, we lick them one by one, cleaning off the evidence. None of us will tell Mum that we ate sweets before lunch.

I think: Dad's son was run over and killed but my sister is alive, I am also very much alive, and Dad shouldn't be so sad anymore.

23.
Mum to Dad: I've just been at the hairdressers and I'm incensed! You've no idea! Rosita knows she's having twin girls and she says she wants to give them the same names as our daughters.

Dad to Mum: This is what happens when you go around saying only you chose the names. You, you, it's all about you.

22.
What would you like most of all? I ask Mum to ask me. You never ask me that. She says: What would you like most of all? A bicycle and *Gone with the Wind*. She buys me the bicycle. In the book she writes: From your Mum, with lots and lots of love. In two separate arguments, she

takes away the presents and gives them to my sister. She crosses out my name in the dedication and writes in my sister's. My sister takes them. She lends them to me.

21.

Mum: Girls, your brother is going to live in another country. We're all going to take him to the airport next Saturday.

My brother: I'll have you to visit so you can see where I live.

My sister: Are you really leaving?

Me: Why are you leaving?

My brother: I'm going to pick apples and oranges over the summer. Then I'm going to travel around Europe. I'll send you loads of photos.

What I hear: I'll send you photos because I'm leaving home.

Dad says nothing. He doesn't mention his son again.

We take pictures with my brother at the check-in desk. Dad takes the photo.

At school they ask us to draw our family, and out of all the colours I choose black. I draw just one man, with a moustache.

Who is it, your brother or your dad? One of them's missing, the teacher says.

20.

In winter I throw stones against bus windows. I break quite a few. The drivers come after me. I hide in the bakery. In summer during carnival I throw water bombs from up on the roof. The drivers ring the doorbell to my house. The bell sounds like something urgent. Mum denies everything.

19.
I collect notepaper decorated with mottos. My favourite has this printed on it: 'He that reads will someday seek to write.'

18.
Atheists are always damned, Mum says to Dad. She gives him a prayer card showing the Divine Mercy. Ask him for something, ask for it in faith. Dad never prays, but he does take us to the Church of Jesus, Mary and Joseph on Sundays and waits for us out in his car until we can *go in peace.* When the priest asks for volunteers to give the first reading, I always offer. He speaks to me in the sacristy. He asks me to read for everyone because adults are moved by children. I modulate my voice to create a special effect, at least among the believers in the first few rows. When I return to my pew, a few old ladies smile at me as if at a favourite granddaughter. I think: if someone comes in with a machine gun right now, I will leap in front of the priest and die for him so that everyone says: That girl is a saint.

17.
In '86 Mum goes to Italy for three months; her first husband has died. The day we go to pick her up from the airport, she's not there. Dad, my sister and I feel abandoned. Orphans for real. Did the plane come down? we ask Dad. She eventually lands the next day. Mum and Dad kiss each other on the mouth when they see each other. This kiss is much better than any present.

We've waited nine years for it! My sister says: You see? They do love each other. I'm going to study hard and I'll be the best so they never split up.

16.
6 p.m.

My sister and I are watching television in Dad's room. We're alone in the house. The telenovela 'Wild Rose' is about to start. We sing: *Rosa Salvaje, soy yo...* We adore Verónica Castro. She doesn't have a family, but someone takes care of her, promises her a home. I say to my sister: I wish she was our mother.

Yeah, me too.

15.
Watch out for men, girls: they always see you as a hole. Your father always saw me as a hole.

14.
At the youth club, a boy takes me to the Statue that Weeps Blood. It's on the first floor. On the ground floor is a basketball court and there's a game on. I like how the players' shoes sound when they screech to a halt; cars and sports shoes sound the same when they stop abruptly. Franco surprises me. A kiss on my right eye, another on the cheek, a third – come on, just do it – full on the mouth. When our tongues touch, I wet myself. The warm trickle soaks my leg, lights flash to celebrate a basket, illuminating it all, I don't care one bit, even though I know without knowing it that an awareness has just formed. I go over the kiss at home, in the bathroom. For the rest of my life I will associate the pleasure of urinating with the pleasure of a kiss.

13.
Dad hides his money in the glove compartment of the car. Mum opens the glove compartment. I catch her stealing. We form an alliance in the garage. She buys my silence with fifty stolen soles. Mum is always saying to

Dad: I can't buy anything with your fifty soles. I find the jar where Mum stashes her dollars and take out twenty. I buy ice creams for my whole class. The ten girls who never speak to me are my new best friends. I buy magazines and chewing gum and Chizito crisps for myself. I fantasise: when Mum is dying, I'll kneel down by her bed and tell her the truth. One evening, I move the jar somewhere else.

You can't say anything to me, I tell her, I learned from you.

I stop stealing from her and start stealing from Dad. Mum knows that I steal from Dad.

We frequently come across one another in the garage.

We are civil.

You first, I say.

12.

Eugenia: Your mother pushed me.

Me: Where?

Eugenia: On the stairs up to my room, look, she hit me.

Me: What did you do?

Eugenia: You know that when your Mum gets angry, she gets *angry*.

11.

I count eight religious figures in my parents' room. There are lots more, but I only know how to count to eight. The beauty of an eight is infinite. Eight is everything for now.

This little boy in the photo – who is it? I always look at it, but I've looked so much that it's only now I'm really seeing it. Is it my brother?

It's your other brother. He died when he was three.

Whose child was he?

Your father's, with his first wife.

What first wife?

I've told you Dad was married before, just like I was.

Dad had a son the same age as your son?

Exactly.

And what was he called?

The same as your dad.

I lie face down on the bed. I cry for this brother I will never know, the brother I've just met.

Where is this dead little boy? Does Dad visit him? Does he visit Dad? What did he look like? Who did he look like? Why is he wearing a suit in the picture? Why is he blond when Dad's hair is black? What day was this photo taken? How did he die? How do they know he's dead? And how can Dad love us if his first child is dead? Why does he never talk about him? Why do children die? What if he wanted another son to replace him? One with the same name as him, again.

10.

My first race.

My aunt comes to our house. I learn that she is Our Lady of Injections. My aunt. I feel betrayed. She hugs me hello. Her gesture does nothing to numb my sadness. I bite her hard on the right boob, really hard. I run up to the roof, to the maid's room, I hide under her bed. They look all over the house for me. They give up. I lie down in this bed for the first time. Something in the room explodes in my face: the silence. I want this to be my room. Small and untidy, with a very low ceiling, remote and perfect.

9.

Mum tells the new maid: The girls aren't allowed to watch TV during the week.

On Saturday I get up really early. I go down to the living room. I hide behind the sofa to spy on the maid. She is taking the exercise books off the table, the fruit bowl with its fake fruits: the apple, the pear, the banana, the grapes which are the most realistic imitation. She passes the feather duster over the table. Sneezes and blows her nose on her apron. I creep up behind her. She jumps from the shock. I threaten her: Are you going to let us watch TV or shall I tell my mum that you wipe your nose on your apron?

Every afternoon, *Popeye*, *Krazy Kat*, *Lady Oscar*, *El Chavo del Ocho*, *Wild Rose*. We watch TV with Eugenia; she does the ironing in Dad's room, just as Mum has instructed her to.

8.

We're all in the kitchen. On Sundays we're allowed to watch TV while we eat. *Magnum, P.I.*, *Hawaii Five-0*. Right now, *The Blue Lagoon* is on. The gringos kiss each other; I feel a tingling down there. They all get poisoned and I start to cry. I want them not to die so that I can have that feeling again.

7.

In a moment of distraction, Dad runs over the puppy we've just bought. They tell us: It's better not to have pets, you grow fond of them and then they die.

6.

My sister and I sit on the stairs.

Mum's a real witch, she says. I don't like it when she hits you.

But I run away. I don't cry into my pillow, like you.

Mum jumps out of her hiding place: I am a witch!

What did I tell you?!!!

5.
A note in my exercise book to return signed by Mum:

Your daughter throws a banana in the bin when she thinks no one is watching.

And with so many starving children in the world!

Mum takes a foreign magazine and shows me African children with their bellies all swollen. It's because of them that you must finish all your food. It's because of them you can never throw any of it away.

But they're full, look at their tummies.

No, they've got worms and diseases and they're going to starve to death.

Memories of the aeroplane: This mouthful's for your grandma, this one's for your aunties, this one's for your sister, this one's for your brother, this one's for your daddy, and this one's for all the little angels in heaven. Neeeooooww! Open your mouth. And this really big one is for all the children in Biafra. Open up! I-won't ask-you-again-to-open-your-mouth.

4.
The brass neck on you, Mum!

To heck with me? Well, fuck you, then!

3.
Does anyone know what happens when we mix blue and yellow together?

I'm the first one to put my hand up.

Who knows the answer? Most of my classmates put their hands up too.

The teacher points at me. We're supposed to stand up when we answer. I get to my feet confidently. I usually hate answering in oral exams. Because of my surname, I'm fifth on the list. By the time they get to the S's all the girls either know the answers or can correct their own.

What happens, then? Let's see if you can tell us.

I say: Moldimix.

The whole class laughs, and the teacher tells me: Into the corner, now.

I don't understand why they're laughing at me. My dad puts everything together with Moldimix. He teaches me how to stick a flowerpot or a piece of broken glass or the dragon's foot, or how to patch up the plumbing. Sometimes I feel like I break things so that I can use Moldimix. If you put blue and yellow together you get Moldimix – see how it sticks everything together?

2.

I shower with my sister. We help each other with the lukewarm water in the jug. We call it The Waterfall: I rinse you, you rinse me. She is eight and I am six. The door to the bathroom is open. The shower has no door. From where we are we can see, but no one can see us. My brother is jumping up and down on my parents' bed. My dad yells at him to get down. We want to play too. We climb naked out of the shower and I follow my sister's wet footsteps.

My brother is leaning against the wall on the landing, his arms wide. He has a cut on his eyebrow. He is staring at Dad like you stare at a madman on the street. My dad is about to hurl a bedside table at him. How did he drag it out here so fast? Repressed memory: Did Dad actually shove it right into him?

Dad hurls this at him: You are not my son! You are not my son!

1.

My first memory. Two years old. Nappy down around my knees. Hand. Cot. I scream. Nobody. I slip. Face. They run.

2.

IF ANYTHING EVER HAPPENS TO US

Against all odds, we survived Christmas.

When I arrived at the apartment, Mariano was playing with his present, a battery-operated toy car big enough for him to sit inside. A red hat was slowly slipping down his forehead, covering his eyebrows. He was sweating. Outside, fireworks whistled, some loud and booming, far out of reach; others, glimmers, blackouts, as if struggling to take off and shine, to be part of the festivities. My brother-in-law greeted me with a brief hug and my sister said: You're just in time. I gave her the things we were going to take to the beach. They heated up portions of turkey, apple sauce and Lebanese-style rice in three pans and served them on gold-rimmed plates. The dining table looked inviting.

Not bad, said my brother-in-law.

Mmm, said my sister, the apple sauce has raisins and nuts in. She chewed some more and covered her mouth with her hand: Sorry, it's just that the supermarkets surprise me more and more every day.

Since they bought the apartment and moved in four years ago, a plastic table, like the ones you find in cheap beachfront restaurants, had been the centre of the living room. They'd put a cloth on the table for the first time, one with a picture of an infinite polar winter: a Scandinavian Christmas landscape, at least thirty degrees below zero, with wooden houses on the flanks of the mountains, as if hanging from the slopes. As soon as we'd finished eating, my sister and brother-in-law got up to do the dishes.

Not today, I said.

They stayed in the living room. Squatting in his little car, Mariano was trying to reach the pedals with his hands. How's everything going? my sister asked. I told them about my afternoon. Generic information, nothing private. From time to time my sister said: Yeah. I fell silent because neither of them was responding. They had fallen asleep. On the floor, on the rug that had been my mother's. They looked exhausted. I sat up until midnight with Mariano, watching him in his car. I took off his hat and flung it to one side. Crushed curls tumbled out over his forehead. He looked relieved. The rockets flared, one after another, joyous explosions. My sister and her husband stirred, but slept on. Children are so tiring, I thought. We pressed all the buttons on the little car's dashboard but only managed to turn the little lights and songs on, then off, then on again. And reverse. We laughed as Mariano lurched backwards at a ridiculous speed. His peals of laughter, new to me: two lower teeth in a mouth that still said not a single word, and so much laughter.

Two Christmases ago, my sister and me.

We were walking in my neighbourhood. The buildings, lights on and off. The houses, lights on and off. In a window, a few silhouettes sat talking around a table.

My sister said: There's a family.

Of course, I felt the same thing, but I wasn't going to put it like that.

If you compare two photos, one of my sister a year after she was born and another of Mariano at the same age, they're a carbon copy. Messy blond curls. Thin lips. Round nose. She in black and white; he in colour. The difference lies in the developing technique, the way they've been printed, the borders and the shadows. Time. Mariano. Sensing my sister as I never knew her. She is three years older than me.

I had said two bold things to them: I want to spend Christmas with you both, and I'd like us to go to the beach on the 25th.

My sister said to her husband: Shall we? We haven't been to the beach for five years.

I said that Mariano couldn't have his first birthday without having seen the sea. I divided up tasks. You buy the beach umbrella. I'll take care of the rest.

They were still sleeping on the living room rug. I mixed three ounces of formula with warm water for Mariano and rocked him in my arms, walking up and down the hallway. When he stopped moving and grizzling, I lay him down next to his mother, on his side, so he could feel her warmth.

I slept in the master bedroom. I'd forgotten what it was like. Kingsize bed, mirror on the wall, bedside tables and chest of drawers, all made by Canziani. My brother-in-law's personality. How to describe it? Voluminous? Monumental and old-fashioned? Don't you just love them? he'd asked my sister. I would have gone for a different style, but I like these pieces, too.

My sister woke me: He's put everything in the car and he's waiting for us.

We dressed Mariano quickly, in his first pair of shorts and his first-ever sandals. I left without brushing my teeth. I sat next to him in the car. In the back. His feet stuck out from the baby seat. He seemed to have grown in the night. Whenever he stretched out his legs, they touched the driver's seat.

You can't put that canopy up on the beach. It's not allowed.

It's so my son can crawl around without getting the sun on him. My sister was holding Mariano and she held him up as evidence.

Where does it say that? Show me.

One of the policemen gave a nod. Another took a photocopy from his shirt pocket: Here, sir.

That's ridiculous. It's completely illogical.

My sister said: We're experiencing the worst UV radiation on the planet here.

We don't make the rules, a third policeman said. You can put up a hundred umbrellas, but not a canopy.

On the planet, did you hear me? my sister insisted. Everyone knows that.

So what do we do now? I said. I set the heavy cool box down on the sand. If I were to open it, I'd plunge my head straight down into the ice.

You hire an umbrella from that young man over there. Fifteen soles for the day.

Fifteen soles? That's daylight robbery!

My brother-in-law whistled to the boy with the beach umbrellas and said, in front of all the policemen, You're all in cahoots, aren't you?

My brother-in-law is a lawyer.

He pulled out the pegs, folded up the canopy, and hurled the whole lot down onto the sand, some way off.

My sister and I applied sun cream. We slathered it all over Mariano. Several layers on his face, in the folds on his neck, on his back and legs. Then we curled up under the umbrella, next to my brother-in-law; he had sat down first. Each of us defending our portion of shade. If your feet stay in the sun, they burn to a crisp before you know it.

How much did you pay for the canopy?

I handed my brother-in-law a can of beer.

Four hundred. But I thought we could use it forever. Turns out it's never.

When he'd finished his beer, my brother-in-law took off the little boy's clothes, leaving just his nappy on, and scooped him up. He kissed his cheek a few times and the noise made the child laugh.

When will he start to talk? I asked my sister.

Little boys are always lazier than girls. Just you wait, soon he'll start saying 'No'. 'No' to everything.

With Mariano in his arms, my brother-in-law started to run towards the sea. I grabbed my phone and ran too. The sand burned. We waited at the edge of the water. Mariano was looking all around him, following the indistinct murmur of the bathers and the waves. My brother-in-law held him against his chest. Well aren't you just the cutest little baby? I counted the waves and said: Now! My brother-in-law moved forward, kicking through the foam. The waves shimmered. A golden fish leapt. My brother-in-law's legs, submerged, and Mariano's feet, feeling the cold water for the first time. Too cold. This beach is called The Secret. To get warm you have to run to the water. Dive in and swim blindly, holding your last breath. This is the secret. In all of the photos I took from the shore, Mariano is crying in the sea. His father is laughing.

Take his nappy off, you hear me? my sister called.

Mariano kicked his legs dejectedly, whined, stared with silent eyes. He was giving in. I wished he would speak, would say his first no. A never-ending no. His father was running to the shore, focused on measuring how fierce the sea was; the waves broke hard upon themselves. The bathers laughed and pointed at them. Celebrating the intangible encounter of a child with his first times, with transience.

The sun moved over the beach. A dive, and I swam nearly sixty metres without coming up for breath. I moved underwater with my eyes closed. Something grazed my leg. A rough black fragment, the remains of a plastic bag, its edges ragged and pointy.

I gazed towards the bay and couldn't make anyone out. All the families looked the same. Adults and children. Beneath the same umbrellas, no canopies. Fleeing from the radiation, yet inhabiting the flimsiest atmosphere.

Another secret of this beach is that the further out you swim from the shore, the colder the water is and the stronger the current that drags you towards the rocks. I saw a fishing boat high up on the shore, abandoned. Its back was turned to the sea. From where I was, it looked anchored to the stone. I swam along parallel to the coast. On another beach hundreds of miles from here, my father, a daughter in each hand, was saying to us:

The sea solves everything.

You must never turn your backs on the sea.

If a wave comes, turn to the side and it won't knock you over.

Today is a good day for swimming, I thought. A jet ski passed close to me. It made white waves, new and happy. Smell of petrol.

A bobbing along, a drowsiness, sinking down, floating up. Drowning must be peaceful. It's a death I would choose. Disappearing, face down, your eye sockets empty, and other life forms entering your body through them, as if into underwater houses.

I saw a figure waving a hand from the shore. From the way it moved, I knew it was my sister. A one-of-a-kind gesture in a body without a face. She was certain it was me she was waving at. On this beach there are always more bathers on the sand than in the water. Of course, lots of people say the sea here is treacherous: in my opinion, a sea that's not treacherous is a lake. Isn't the Pacific the most violent ocean of them all? Few of us swim very far. There's a frantic urgency to it, plunging in and moving your arms in cold, open, solitary waters, dark and unbearable, for those who actually enjoy it. As I do.

Listen to me, you can't tell anyone, my sister demanded.

My mother used to hit me. If my father lost his temper, he would hit me, too. Never my sister. Not even once. She didn't protect me, either. But they mollycoddled her and now her whole thing is 'obey and act, obey and silence'. The sea solves everything. It's not true. Each wave cast me out of my parents' arms and left me more exposed to the elements.

We bent the umbrella down over our heads; we slipped around in the sand, chasing the one circle of shade.

My sister said: I want one, too.

And I took pictures of the three of them on the wet sand. The shore spread out, hungry seagulls pecked at the crab holes, a few crabs dodging them, others already flying away in their beaks; the foam crept back and forth, washed clean, melted away; the waves roared, serene and eager; the sky: deep blue, pink, violet. My sister and brother-in-law smiled at the camera. Mariano! I shouted a few times. He never turned around. Held by his father, he was watching the endless coming and going of the waves, his eyes wide and his mouth open.

We had to take the old highway first. About one and a half miles to the tollbooth and the new road.

Mariano was in his seat, dozing, and I was messaging on my phone. I was replying to my best friend; I had invited her to come with us to the beach. She had written back: Not with your brother-in-law there.

When I looked up, the bus was heading straight for us.

You know what you did! You know what you did! You know what you did! He was whacking the windscreen of the bus with the steering wheel lock. I didn't know he had one and had never seen him use it. Not on the steering wheel, or against a person. The windscreen, impervious, and the same words repeated without pause. He ran around to the driver's side and smashed in the side window. He ran back to our car. The conductor leapt out of the bus. My sister gave a cry. A long howl, more animal than human. The conductor heaved up one of the concrete milestones from the side of the road. He held it up above his head.

Hey, there's a baby here! I pointed at the child seat. The conductor couldn't see it. Mariano was invisible.

We were hemmed in by the patrol car with its blue lights flashing and by the bus itself.

The passengers surrounded us.

He tried to kill us!

My brother-in-law pressed a button on the dashboard and wound up the car windows.

He's crazy!

Get him!

They filmed us on their phones. Pressed them up against the windows. My brother-in-law said: If they're going to film me, then I'm going to film them. He grabbed his phone, activated the camera. He panned around from inside the car to outside, including all of us. I put my head down, burying my chin and mouth inside my top. Mariano was sleeping in his seat, his legs dangling.

The policemen got out of their car: Ah, it's you, sir.

My brother-in-law was directing his own film in real time. His face impassive, on the surface. Point-of-view: group shot of scared, angry car passengers, surrounded by scared, angry bus passengers. I couldn't tell who the extras were, us or them.

The bus driver and the conductor leapt down into the road.

Another policeman instructed my brother-in-law to lower his window:

We're going to have to bring you in for questioning, sir.

Under arrest? said my sister.

I said: You're going to jail.

Hand over your license, and then you're going to follow me, with the bus driver, to the police station.

The bus, empty of passengers, escorted us.

I said: You're going to jail. You really are this time.

Come on, said my sister. Do you mind, now's really not the time.

Two large dogs with reddish-brown coats lay panting in the door to the police station. Stretched out, uneasy, their eyes open wide. Labrador crosses (with what?).

I was carrying Mariano.

Their names are Choccie and Fakedog, said the officer on duty.

The policeman – the chief, apparently – announced that he would now proceed with the incident report.

Where were you hit?

Here.

Impossible, shouted the bus driver. It's on the side, and that's an old vehicle. There'd be paint.

Did they hit you?

No, they didn't.

Do you, or your family, have any physical injuries?

No, but –

Do you have any injuries? Yes or no.

No.

The driver's turn. A round face, with brows like balls of fluff about to float away. His eyes, deep-set and black, like an owl's. On the palm of his left hand there are cuts.

Right, said the chief police officer, as you can see, it's clear that the windscreen has been struck in several places.

That's going to cost, said the driver.

Shards and fragments of glass from the car's side window were still falling onto the road. They lay glinting in single file under the door, as if someone had gathered them up to make a stained-glass window.

I went over to the conductor and said: Thank you for not throwing that thing at us.

He said: I saw my driver bleeding and I flipped.

We entered the police station. The dogs didn't move.

A chair for the lady.

What a sweet little boy.

They sat me down in front of the television, which murmured away at a very low volume.

A low wall divided the television area from the work area. The work area was in a corner, small and neglected.

The chief of police sat down at a desk in front of a typewriter and said to my brother-in-law, the driver and the conductor: Take a seat.

They all sat down.

I'm neutral. You either resolve this here, quickly, for good, or you'll end up in court at a long, boring trial.

The conductor took his phone out of his pocket: I'm calling the company lawyer.

We'll take minutes, in that case.

Sound of a typewriter. How long had it been since I'd heard one?

On the stage, King Kong ripped off the chains that bound him. An imitation jungle surrounded him. The blonde actress they'd found for him was a replacement. He'd just discovered the substitution. He yanked up the seats in the theatre and lurched out onto the streets of New York. He destroyed car after car. He was looking for his woman.

On top of the TV, this typed note:

THE TV MUST *ALWAYS* BE LEFT
ON THE NEWS CHANNEL
NOT COMPLYING WITH THIS RULE
IS CONSIDERED A SERIOUS OFFENCE.
THE SUPERINTENDENT

Mariano wasn't watching the television. There was no television in his parents' apartment. He was hypnotised by the purple fly swatter one of the policemen had. The man noticed Mariano watching him and started pretending to swat flies on his desk. The contrast of the purple with his green uniform. That must have been it.

Thwack. Mariano laughed. Thwack.

Thwack.

I am neutral, the superintendent had said. Did he really say that?

I noted that my sister was in the doorway of the police station watching everything.

Bring the weapon, sir.

Now?

Right now.

Thwack. Mariano chuckled in my arms.

What a sweet little boy, eh? A real cutie.

On the day he was born, I said his name to him for the first time, picked him up and carried him around the corridors of the clinic. A little girl came up to me, asked if she could see him. She looked at him for a long time and said: So sweet, is he new? Of course, I thought the same thing and I told her. Yes, he's new.

My brother-in-law left the police station, followed by my sister.

The blonde actress, the real one, found King Kong in the street. He picked her up in his fist, held her in such a way that her body disappeared, just head and feet, and ran as apes run, freely and angrily, and they slid around on a frozen lake. They laughed, beauty and beast, staring into each other's kind eyes, not cracking the ice despite all their weight on it. Until someone shoots at them.

Mariano was getting bored. He was sweating. I kissed his damp head. He squirmed.

On the day he was born, my sister said: If anything ever happens to us…

I said: Shush, you mustn't think about things like that.

It's really important to me that you think about it.

I regretted having shushed her and tried to calm her down: OK, but we should put it in writing and sign it, the three of us.

I got up and went to sit in the other free chair, next to the driver and the conductor. I'm really sorry, I said. They looked at me and nodded.

My brother-in-law placed the steering wheel lock on the desk. The brand was printed in white lettering on red paint: Hercules II. The sound of the typewriter again.

My brother-in-law looked at me. Give him here, he said. I hand Mariano over.

My sister was still in the doorway. Again. Near the

dogs with their funny names. I liked how they had non-scary names. They looked like they deserved them.

Sir, the superintendent said to my brother-in-law: You have committed a crime, and that crime is called assault.

No one reacts like that without good reason, my friend, the superintendent said to the driver. You must have done something.

The driver said: That's not what happened.

My brother-in-law passed Mariano back to me. Then he bent down, levelling his eyes with the official's: We should settle this like men, chief. I don't have time for all the formalities.

My brother-in-law, to the driver: You know what you did. But how much do you reckon a windscreen is worth? How much is your car window worth? How much is your hand worth?

The driver and the conductor glanced at each other. The policeman at the desk still had the fly swat in his hand. The police station was neither clean nor dirty. But there were no flies. Perhaps there used to be. Some other summer. The Secret is my favourite beach. I can't recall a summer when there were flies.

My brother-in-law reached into his pocket. He turned to my sister. She came over. She took the wallet. We listen: Go and take out a thousand.

Come with me, my sister said to me.

No, it's too far. You go and I'll stay here with Mariano.

Where's the cashpoint?

At the petrol station, I said.

Very sweet baby you've got, the policeman with the fly swat said to me.

I wanted to reply that I was his aunt. That it's much better to be the aunt than the mother. I said nothing, of course.

My brother-in-law said: She's my sister-in-law.

As my sister walked to the cashpoint, I imagined what she must be thinking. My sister was thinking that this day at the beach had cost them one thousand four hundred soles, the most expensive day at the beach of their lives.

Inside the police station there was nothing else to do but wait.

As if by tacit agreement, we all turned in our seats towards the TV. We watched King Kong holding out at the top of the Empire State building. He hadn't lost yet. The police station was a cinema theatre.

My sister returned with the money.

My brother-in-law divided it up: eight hundred for the driver, two hundred for the police station.

You sign here and you: here.

Do you want a copy? the superintendent asked the driver. You can get copies in the shop around the corner.

There's no need, said my brother-in-law. We've settled this like men now. He was wrong, and so was I.

Apologise to him, said the policeman.

He hasn't apologised yet, said the conductor.

My brother-in-law clapped the driver on the arm. Not looking the man in the eyes, he said: OK – look after that hand, and drive safely.

He took the document, folded it and put it in his wallet.

Let's go.

I'm trying to save on the food shopping, even, and then you go and spend all that money in just one day, said my sister.

Mariano slept on in his seat.

I thought they were going to put you in jail, I said.

We could have died, said my brother-in-law.

But we didn't, I said.

One day at the beach and all that money, said my sister. I can't believe it. Do you have anything for the toll?

Are you asking me? I asked.

Yes, you.

None of this would have happened if you two could drive.

I say: I don't want to drive because I'm afraid of crashing.

My sister: Me too. You know that.

Me: I really thought they were going to put you in jail.

My sister: He's right, they could have killed us. He was on our side of the road. He was right in front of us. Right here.

Me: But it didn't happen.

My brother-in-law: The worst thing was I couldn't even swerve, because there was a whole load of people at a bus stop just to the right of us. Did you see that? No, of course you didn't. None of it was up to me. Just think – with Mariano there.

I looked at my nephew. His curls ruffled by the wind. It's strange: Awake he looks like his mother; asleep, like his father.

What would his first words be? Would I miss them?

On the day he was born, my best friend said to me: The best thing that could happen to that child is that one day you adopt him.

My sister turned to look at her son, grabbed his foot and gave it a shake: He's such a deep sleeper, he's completely dead to the world. Wouldn't you love to be that young again!

They were about to lob a piece of concrete this big at us. What if it had landed on him? As soon as I said this, I realised that not for anything in the world would I be one year old again and live through everything I've lived through before now, especially with my memory. In my family it's a case of who forgets things first. I wondered what age it is when the brain starts to form memories, to replace them with others, to reject them. Were today's images accumulating like sediment in Mariano's head?

My sister: Right, enough, let's talk about something else, please. Let's not think about this. Could it have been worse? Yes, but it wasn't. Right. When you can, love, pull over, seeing as the baby's sleeping. I'm dying for the toilet.

3.

THE COLOUR OF ICE

León said: We're going to Ticlio.

I said: We've never gone that far. And regretted it immediately. I wasn't going to be the coward of the group yet again. If someone wants to see snow for the first time, they go to Ticlio, it's the closest you can get to Sweden here, my father used to say.

I'll be waiting for you here in ten minutes. Bring whatever you want.

Juan Enrique came back quickly, as did I. He was holding something black in his hands – something dead? He showed it to me. It fires blanks, he said.

It looked like a toy, the pieces badly fitted together, Chinese plastic. The one decent-looking thing about it was the grip.

I said: It's shit, Juane.

Juane: Hey, a little respect, please: my aunt pointed this thing at me when I was ten. She was smiling when she did it. I was shaking all over, you guys have no idea. We were driving in her car, someone cut her up, and she aimed at the drivers: You're fucked, now you're really gonna die, you piece of shit. Afterwards she laughed, 'that's how things work in this country, kiddo.'

León: And she was right. I brought my old man's beers. We'll have to replace them, last time he nearly…

Me: Let's see, Juane, give it here.

I sat in the back, with the gun and the beers. I've always known my place. I'm the one who observes everything from the back seat.

We took León's father's car. His father goes by bus out to the provinces on weekends. What kind of business does he do? We all put in money for petrol; I stole mine from a jar of soap. My mother's money smells of clean things. The highway. The only unpredictable thing about it is how often people try to cross it without using the bridges. Drivers have to keep their headlights on at all hours. We love and hate the highway. We grew up learning from it. We see it when we wake up, visible between the curtains, without a landscape. We see it when we get back home, with its horizon of long sunsets. Or obscured at any time by the fog.

We all went to different schools. We'd met one February during the holidays. León was about to turn nine and his family had organised a barbecue for him in their new neighbourhood. Our fathers clap each other on the back, do little favours for each other. They have us round on weekends. Saturdays are ours, just as afternoons at León's house used to be, after lunch. We played friendlies with stones, the goalposts our steadily moulting exercise books. Gooooal! Losing the ball, a tragedy. Hence our attitude towards the stones. We could replace them for other, more spectacular ones. Pain-free losses. And if water was involved, the street was a carnival. Give children a little bit of water and they'll invent an ocean. Our favourite game, 'killem'. We'd smash the ball hard against the backs of ugly girls; we were quite ugly ourselves, too, ugly boys in progress, with suppurating spots and all that sort of thing. We had a rule we said aloud: You can only look at your own girl.

We've respected it until now.

I could always run the highest up a wall. A precise footprint beats whoever spits or pisses the furthest, that's the rule. León and Juane still persuade me: Hey, that wall's pretty white.

The soles of my shoes print lopsided graffiti, until someone snaps and paints several layers over the top. Once I was caught doing it. It was awful. They sprayed me with a hose. Pig-headed from humiliation, I carried on kicking at the wall of the house as if this family were the enemy. It was a period when we cried seldom and felt a great deal. Venturing out, going back home – our dynamic. How would we cope living anywhere else, accustomed as we were to repetition? It's not good to get used to things. It doesn't matter how old you are, boredom drugs you.

The requirement to do something in order to be someone. We're sick of the shouting. There is no silence. Sick of shooting at the same guys on the computer, sick of the endless bursts of gunfire, of running out of lives or ammo, of the everyone-against-everyone. Sometimes reading calms me down. But a book always ends.

I said: What if we do what your aunt did, Juane? If a car cuts us up, we aim at it.

León: ...

We say: Shut the fuck up, but we need music for that. Right, guys? My old man doesn't care that the radio's broken; how can he live without music? He says the voices in his head are enough. Crazy fucker.

Juane tapped at the cracked dashboard: And the speedometer's just as crazy as he is, lucky for us.

León would never let us drive his father's car. He knows what he's doing. We're way too absentminded.

Here came the roadside altars, set apart from one another, multiplied. Wordlessly, I pointed one out. It was León who said: That one's huuuge, it looks like a house. See those bridges? Every mayor was asked to pay for one and now that they've got them – useless.

Dying like a dog? Idiots!

Juane's voice. I'm intrigued by the roadside altars, a scaled-down city that connects the dead to the living. I picked up the cans of beer, started to open them. Want one? Here you go. I stared at the gun resting at my side. I would have killed for this toy as a kid. The beers on the highway anaesthetise me, freezing me, like the air that seems to buzz all alone in the back seat. I grabbed the gun and pointed at a telegraph pole, bang, out from the muzzle, at another pole, bang, they looked like beaten men, bang, at lots and lots of other poles. The cars, the buses, the motorbikes, the street sellers' trikes were all stubbornly keeping a safe distance from one another. It was exasperating. We needed something extraordinary: a container truck skidding off the road, a procession of sheep, a cardboard box slipping off the back of a lorry, a hailstorm. As if, just at the break in the cartography, one of us were to say:

Now I really feel like the journey's begun.

Juane said we'd forgotten to bring anything to eat. It was true, my stomach was growling. León was driving with one hand. The highway, with no traffic lights, laid out like a prize: residential and commercial areas would gradually grow more and more spaced out. All clear – in the summer we'd go hours without being able to move. Up above, like circuits of smoke, dense clouds. A day that is night-time, I thought. Uneven roofs hold metal-framed bulls laden with fireworks; if they go off by mistake, they whizz around, euphoric, bouncing off roofs, pointing with their horns, with the whole of their sinewy bodies, skeleton and bulk, until finally charging with their pointed, smoking heads. The walls on either side of the highway, a beginning and an end, painted with the slogans of mayoral hopefuls. Lots of surnames sounded unfamiliar to me; their promises, less so. Other walls had threatening biblical quotes, ending with the number of the verse. Somewhere, between the highway and a bridge, a discovery livened up the route for me. Only I saw the phrase on the wall:

Children are the only privileged ones.

I even turned my head to follow it. Childhood. My mother used to say: Getting through childhood is to survive the worst of all tsunamis. I didn't understand this. What could have happened to her? If she broke a glass, she'd throw the shards into the dustbin without first wrapping them in newspaper. The binman will cut his fingers, Mum! The risk is part of the job, she would reply. Her favourite painting: *The Destruction of Pompeii*. A print of it still hangs in the living room at home. From the reflection of light on the water, the calm hours of the sea, I used to think it was a lost kingdom, Atlantis or something similar. I only saw the destruction when I found out what the title was. My mother is the last stenographer at her work: she is secretary to the manager at a bank. In her diary, the names, the addresses, the to-do lists and the – how should I know? – are symbols no one else can comprehend. Secrets are what make us interesting. I stole a photo from an exhibition. The image of a woman reading. It was hanging from a hook, it seemed so easy. I walked over to the entrance, where the security guards were watching videos on a computer with the sound off. I sneaked out like a professional thief, holding it in my hand. I still have the photo; once I told a girl about the theft and she kissed me.

Juane asked me for another beer. I opened him a can. León said: Did you hear it's the coldest winter in thirty years? And we're going to Ticlio.

I said that lots of people were barricading themselves in with this cold; it's so dull, much better to hibernate.

León: That's so over the top, the problem's the grey sky, that stormy sky without any storm.

Me: The other day I read that the happiest countries in the world are the ones with the highest suicide rates.

Juane sipped at his can of beer: That makes no sense.

I said: But there's no relationship between a city where it always rains and suicide.

Who wants to kill themselves if they're happy? Juane said. Right now, beer is the only thing making me happy. We laughed. He started to burp: A, B, C, D, E, F, G, H. We copied him. Nowadays we struggled to finish the alphabet. When you have to make an effort, something has been lost, or not.

We passed under another bridge.

You think anyone's ever jumped off that one? said León.

I don't think so, Mr Philosopher, I said.

Open me another beer and don't fuck with me.

I'll open it quick as running up a wall, just you watch.

You think you're so clever, don't you? León's eyes smiled in the rear-view mirror. His voice went on, cocky: Reading all day long – for what?

To know about how Tokyo has boredom rooms.

Juane said: Boredom's the same everywhere. If I could travel I'd prove everyone on the planet sleeps in a bed. Even if the bed is made of ice covered in sealskin, it's still a bed, isn't it? I've always wondered how beds went viral before the internet.

You can tell you're bored, Juane: travel is what let ideas migrate, I said. Just shut up, for the sake of the seals.

And at that moment we drove past a market.

León slowed. Lettuces, tomatoes, carrots, sweetcorn, cabbages, balanced in little mounds on broad tables. A number of sacks sat on the ground (no need to open them); the market was dead. Chickens ran around, mad and free, not one of them approaching the highway. No one had taught them how to avoid it. Their curiosity was content to just peck at the same flat ground.

OK, give me the gun, León asked.

He aimed with his left hand. He carried on driving with his right, making sure we stayed in our lane.

Do you think that old woman's happy? León's eyes spoke to me in the rear-view mirror. Juane glanced at León. A silence.

Which one?

That one there, the fruit seller. Old raisinface.

How do I know? I don't know her.

No way is she happy – take a good look at her. If she doesn't want to be there, so be it.

León's body slammed back against the seat. A harsh ringing. His arm returned to normal. My lips moved without articulating anything. As if I'd forgotten language and its effects. León fixed his eyes on me. In the mirror we were together.

I tried to shout: Son of a bitch, stop the car! I'm getting out. Except this buzzing and shaking. If I'd been able to open the door and jump.

I don't know about you, but I'm bored. Bored of everything.

Me too, said Juane. I'm tired of being tired.

Me too, I said, but killing someone? What the fuck?

Don't exaggerate.

But León.

My friends' voices sounded ghostly to me.

You want to get out here? Tell me honestly. Is that

what you want? Jump out now, I'm not slowing down, man. Not for you. Not for anybody.

The car reeked of gunpowder. The smell of fireworks at Christmas. The whole block, a lightly toxic cloud above the trees, pavements, walls, houses. They can burn your fingers, chase you up to your front door, turn your trousers into a vertical fuse; the risk was fun.

You guys would never do that even if you were drunk, I said. Who are you? I want my friends back.

No, we're not drunk at all. That's the point.

León passed the gun to Juane. Juane turned around to look at me, a senseless resolve glittering in his eyes.

What? I tried to shout.

Juane put it back where it had been, next to me. I looked at it for all of two seconds. León, both hands facing forwards, steering wheel and highway. One of Juane's hands dangled out of the window, playing with the air, the wind pushing it backwards. Towards me. Slack, incapable of holding anything. When had this collusion started? In the sea, in the hollow of a steel pole, in a forgotten net, fish build things, they have a house in every sunken prow. Our friendship had survived all spaces. My friends are a lump of ice floating in dark waters. I failed to see it coming.

We moved along, passing huge posters promising sun the whole year round. They came before restaurants closed for winter, narrow houses (a single block of dirty cement, walls of earth and lime). I thought about the woman. It was a mystery whether she was alive. León had known that the gun was real.

Everyone had known it except me.

If I hadn't shot her, why the guilt? That's what can't be fixed, I said to myself, and it comes from somewhere very far off. I racked my brains. What could happen to me? What was eluding me? At last I said: What if the police stop us, what will we say? Who does the gun belong to?

There aren't any police cars around here, for starters Can you see one? No one's following us. It's fine.

We got out of the car.

Instead of snow, ice.

Leave the windows open so they don't get misted up.

What about the keys?

Leave them here. It'll be fine.

We had waited years for this sign. And now here it was in front of us.

It was obsolete. Another railway junction in China had surpassed Ticlio in altitude, and I muted my 'I knew it'.

All this ice. As a boy I'd put my tongue onto the ice at the bottom of the freezer and it had got stuck. My mother had pulled my head back. I had a pain in my tongue, a strange pain, I don't suppose too many people can have felt such a thing.

Something white was glittering up on the peaks, though. Unreachable. The shocking blue of a sky exploding on the mountain. We were shivering. We blew onto our cupped hands (I knew it); by this point, warming them up like that was a gesture in transition, the only thing we shared. I felt glad that neither Juan Enrique nor León was speaking. The tourists in their centipede lines. Can you take another? This one's got your fingers in it.

The sign continued to lie and they believed it, words sustained by words.

What do you want? I said to myself. They would never ask me this question – they continued to blow on their numb old men's hands – nor would my parents. Or anyone.

I felt the urge to go back to the car and get the gun. To shoot at the ice, a bullet for each one of us. To smash it, to kick it. Shoes like the blades of ice skaters. Watch legs fall into the freezing water, see trousers without bodies go by. When people fall into a hole in the ice, they always try to climb out in a different place to where the accident occurred. It's a mistake. The strongest ice is the part that held all that weight before it cracked. We couldn't even agree on how we'd met. At a barbecue, yes. The time, the details, the weather, what we said to each other – what were they? We had argued about this once. It could also be that I never forgot.

They won't remain intact either.

I wound down the window. Warmed up the engine. They ran over to me.

They looked at me.

I stopped seeing them.

I stretched my legs out effortlessly. I imagined reaching the jungle for the first time. The sun breaking through the clouds and the clouds like children's arms encircling each other. The vegetation. Where am I now? and the strangers replying with anything, just for the sake of replying.

4.

ALASKA

Early cartographers, when alluding to unexplored territories, used to write on their maps:

HERE BE DRAGONS.

If I were a cartographer, I would rewrite a detail on the family map:

HERE BE ~~DRAGONS~~ ICEBERGS.

Belén

I don't know the year. The name. The months spent travelling. Or if there was a war.

My paternal grandfather, settled in Arequipa, owner of the first textile mill on the continent, demands photos. Belén is looking for another virgin. The girl who will become my grandmother, Hortensia, is thirteen years old. The merchant families exchange camels as a dowry.

Eleven children. All the boys – eight of them – are given Salvador as their second Christian name.

Register of Deaths: one dropped by the midwife,

another run over by a tram, a girl from sun stroke.

Hortensia crippled from testifying three times. She was bed-bound when she had my father. He is the last.

Pinzolo

1914. Margherita digs graves. There are ten bodies. She is thirteen years old.

1943. In an area that once belonged to Austria and will become Italian territory again, she makes a decision.

She flees with Guglielmo to Tuxtla, and they work in the silver industry. They migrate to Potosí; silver mines again. They migrate to Lima, he as foreman of the Cerro de Pasco Copper Corporation. They buy twenty hectares; eventually they will sell the land, fleeing agrarian reform.

My maternal grandparents. Rita and Guillermo.

Five children. My mother is the youngest. Name of a Spanish queen.

Arequipa

A revolution against General Odría's government brews in the classrooms of the Colegio de la Independencia.

Vali, inaptly nicknamed the Turk, is in the fourth year of secondary school. Elected student leader by pure chance, impervious to danger, he is among the first to pull up paving stones from the square outside, hurl them at the police and hunker down behind the school walls. Mothers come and throw over blankets, newspapers, tins of tuna, water. One day, a death. Four days, four deaths. With a criminal record, unable to work or study, Vali travels to the United States. He serves in the army.

How was I to know that just four days would determine my whole life? he told me more than fifty years later.

Baltimore

Between Korea and Vietnam, he dodges battles. Action stations. Hauling himself through dust and barbed wire, he eats worms, survives. Paratrooper jumping out at ten thousand feet. The enemy is everywhere. If he makes a mistake in training, the punishment is the kitchen. He fries potatoes, bacon, makes gravy. A camouflaged question becomes routine: When is it, the next war? Will it be his turn? Vali has a wife, a son, a house, an Oldsmobile.

Somewhere in the Mediterranean

It is carnival time on board the *Amerigo Vespucci*. Isabel meets Marco and Pietro, dances the voyage with them. She has been sent to Italy, far from suitors. Men shout all kinds of things at her. Her parents would entrust her with a shotgun whenever they went out: If anyone comes in through that door, you shoot. As soon as they arrive, she marries Pietro. On their wedding night they sleep on a bench outside a hotel in Pinzolo, still waiting for their marriage certificate.

Snow falls.

They are eighteen years old.

Fairbanks

At thirty degrees below zero, Vali drives a tank across the repeated night. His friends joke around, showing off their membership cards to The Frozen Club. The enormous machine stops, fails to start again. Vali lights and keeps alight a bonfire; he saves them all until they are rescued, the ventilated tank preventing their death. He is allowed to go home for a while. It will be a surprise. To be welcomed as if he'd finished a test, as if everything were the same, just as he'd longed for every day. He finds his wife with his best friend. His two-year-old son in the same room. He smashes up the house. How did you do it? With a machete, until there was nothing left. He kidnaps the boy. He will never return to the United States.

Trento

Pietro is given the job of official photographer for the Italian embassy in Peru. Isabel is six months pregnant. They live in Miraflores. They become the first importers of Fuji film. They hang black and white portraits out of the window of their house; everyone has to look up as they drive around the Gutiérrez roundabout.

Little Pietro is born.

Pietro senior travels to Cuzco. When she goes to meet him there, Isabel discovers his prostitute lover. She returns to Lima alone to look after the baby. *Suo marito* goes back to Italy. Forever. She works as executive secretary at the Mining Bank. In the summer of 1986, she will stay in Italy for three months with little Pietro, burying her first husband. The child claims his inheritance: one final migration. When Isabel dies, he will not be with her before, during or afterwards.

Lima

Father and son live in a seventh-floor apartment in La Victoria. Vali teaches English at the Naval Academy. One morning he sends his son out to buy bread with the boy's older cousin: I'll watch you from up here. Vali cries out, a cry that comes out mute, smashes the window with his fists. It's too late. He will watch his son get run over by a truck transporting toilet paper. The driver is sixteen years old. He will not go to jail. Vali tears down the seven flights of stairs. The boy dies in his arms. From Baltimore his ex-wife files charges against him for abduction and murder.

Camaná

I'd have beautiful children with you!

Who is this idiot? Isabel follows this voice up to the roof terrace. Vali is shaving, stripped to the waist; bruise-like kisses on the neck, the back. They detest each other. The families spend their summers playing cards. Their friends speculate: such a beautiful couple should appreciate each other; they're a South American carbon copy of Gena Rowlands (in *A Woman Under the Influence*) and Omar Sharif (in *Doctor Zhivago*). Isabel never accepts an invitation to dance; she feels her way forward with monosyllables. One night she will send a message: I am ill. She doesn't go to meet him. He will go to her with champagne.

She: You lost your son. I have one the same age.

Much later, someone referring to the two of them: Disaster attracts disaster.

Lima

Until the smoke inhabited their bodies, the doctors said. The wooden box that is my father is in the house. My sister couldn't see a way to keep our mother with her. We share them out, as they do with us. It is difficult to get rid of ashes; to make them vanish is effortlessly bold (a consistency between matter and nothing). We discuss throwing them into the sea at El Silencio, where we managed to spend two final summers. I surprised my father: there are chairs with beers, crunchy seafood *jalea* with shade; sitting down, he dwindled in size. On Sundays we coaxed our mother there. We took the dogs. They're still alive. I took pictures of them with their legs in the air, little horses, curious and desiring, pure hot blood.

And yet in the warm waking creature
is the care and burden of a great sadness.

Since it too always has within it what often overwhelms us –
a memory

RAINER MARIA RILKE,
EIGHTH DUINO ELEGY, 1923

Illness robs memory of its dignity, repeating a repetition. Isn't the central theme in Agatha Christie's work the fact that there are always other ways to recount the same mystery? My parents, even now, lymph nodes. My parents, eyelids that I shut.

In the polar regions, the permafrost – this is what ice that never melts is called – impedes burials. At the same time, nothing rots. If someone wishes to look for the strain of flu that killed half the world in 1918, there it is, in the memory of the ice.

As a boy I looked at dozens of negatives before choosing which ones to develop, which ones to go back to. Vali and Isabel were like this. We had to give photographs to the funeral parlour. When they were retouched, their anger disappeared. Smiles were sketched with cotton wool. The fake smiles horrified me; a mouth is what says: this is where a unique being fed itself, loved, answered back, hummed a tune.

Can I say this impossible thing? The day my parents were born was the day I felt the most relieved.

When an iceberg calves, life begins to form around it. The distance travelled comes back, establishing a new cycle. From ice waves to the Krakatoa effect. A fragmented story – none is linear – emerging.

Alaska, in Aleut, one of the Eskimo-Aleut languages: *The object towards which the action of the sea is directed.*

5.

THAT HORSE

I was on land belonging to a grandfather (not mine).

All around the grandfather, a group of men moved busily about.

I had got up and dressed all by myself and left the house.

They were looking at something.

The black horse, on the ground, its jaw oddly set, its hair all messy and wig-like. Drunken eyes. They glanced at me for a second.

One of them said: Just look at its leg, poor thing.

Another remarked that there was only one solution. There's nothing for it, better do it now and put it out of its misery.

They discussed its virtues. It liked the mud. Galloping off for the sake of it. Running long distances. They said it had fallen into the ditch. It's the ditch that's broken it, Señor, someone said, I saw it happen.

The gun appeared, passed from hand to hand. Black, horse-coloured. The same way friends pass a beer glass around and tip the frothy dregs onto the floor.

Let's put an end to this once and for all, the grandfather said, eventually. He aimed at the horse as I turned around and, just like that, my back to them.

Towards the house where my parents slept.

I ran.

I heard wails. From the horse, not one.

Let's see, nothing of mine had died. Just my shoes (my feet were growing fast).

In the house, my parents were snoring.

I let them sleep. I sat down on the floor in front of their bed. I let them sleep.

Right, enough, I went over, tugged at the bedclothes.

Let's eat some breakfast first. They had eggs and filter coffee, fruit. They read the newspaper, discussed the news. The price of chicken is getting higher and higher, what are we going to do? A baby had bitten a snake. A restaurant had been shot up at point-blank range.

I asked and they explained.

I said: And the horse was, at pelt-blank range.

What?

The horse, with its black pelt. The one they said I could have a go on just yesterday.

And my father left the room.

My mother said: Hang on, darling, I'll come with you, wait a minute.

Leaning against the wall I waited. I saw mud on my trainers. Mud from running around the smallholding, from jumping over ditches, from climbing up onto the edge of the well when no one was looking, from sitting and dangling my feet into its mouth, from lowering down the bucket until the rope hung, free fall, and the water rang out, then pulling it back up empty.

My parents came back. They had seen what I had.

My forehead, my eyes. They kissed me as if I were going to.......... or as if they were going to.......... But I didn't know about that, about death, I wasn't going anywhere.

Let's go to the market, sweetheart, buy some tasty things to eat. Whatever you want!

We left the house via another door, new to me.

They squeezed the avocados. Don't touch the produce. They listened out for the stone rattling in their ears. No. You hear that? It's not ready yet. A ripe one, please. For eating today.

I went over to where the grey-skinned chickens were hanging, a separate aisle to the fruit, the vegetables, the dry goods. It smelled different there: a smell that made no attempt at persuasion. The bones in a separate bag, the wings submerged in their soy sauce, the pig heads impaled far from their bodies, the ribs in the Monday night lentils. There was enough there to put it all together and create a whole new animal.

In the aisles someone called my name. Once again, I wondered why this name was mine, just mine, even though other girls were called the same as me.

They came over to get me. They handed me my bag of fruit so I wouldn't forget why we were there. One by one, eating up the blackberries. So delicious. My hands all purpled. See my hands?

It'll come off with water. But you've already wiped them on your trousers. Can't you stay clean for just one day?

Leave her, we'll be home soon, you said it yourself, it'll come off with water.

Our things were left out on the smallholding, they were ruined. My cars that screeched away with their tyres in the air and crashed and kept on going, my little toy animals, the stones I had collected, the threads from the rope for the well.

My red dress, Mum said, I used to love that dress.

Damn it – my new lighter, I don't believe it. My father.

I said: My little farm.

My parents looked at each other. We've been thinking – do you want a little brother? Would you like that?

As if I could see them: the figures of the father, the mother, the little children, *mooo*, said the gate, the cow, the donkey, the little horse. A nativity scene the whole year long. It was mine and now it wasn't.

On other mornings I went back to the market, where the city and my memory overlapped. The chickens in the killing cone; beaks down, they bleed out with one sharp cut, kicking through the last tremor, hanging from their hooks like pairs of yellow trousers, flabby pockets, atrophied buttons, opposite grey fish with their eyes forever open, crabs still uselessly jabbing at the ice, clams half-closed in reptilian winks. The feathers float alone, the steam is murky, thick and liquid, water running hotly down into cracks. Me? Sitting, taking notes on the extermination: two hundred and seventy-four chickens, the first morning. The heart, a trawl net in deep waters, hunts without knowing what it's caught: the same things in different places or different things in the same places.

Years later, my hand would hold (how could anyone have known; they still said of me: She is innocent) necks sliced into words that came too late.

That horse.

I had loved it.

It moved lightly with its profound face.

Eyes that looked at me for a moment.

In its shining eyes I saw defeat.

6.

WHERE THE HUNTS TAKE PLACE

Why the hell do we have dogs? said the father. They jump right up to my elbows. They don't even bark! An ambulance goes by and they howl like crazy.

He asked for a list of possible culprits.

A monkey, said the eldest son.

No. Too easy; the youngest son.

A child, the mother declared.

Yeah, right, a crafty little kid who gets up really early, steals our fruit and attacks us while singing 'Bang Bang', quipped the father. And he did a little dance on the spot and sang: *Bang Bang, I shot you down, Bang Bang, you hit the ground, Bang Bang, that awful sound*... The boys were about to finish off the chorus; the father silenced them with a look. When I die, he used to say, it won't be food I'll miss the most, it'll be music. They all trooped out of the house. They smelled the walls. The dogs sniffed, too, moved back. The younger son bravely ran his finger over the surface, tasted it; it's only fruit.

Darling? said the mother.

What is it? the father.

Yesterday I read that Alain Delon said: My whole life is there, in the graves where my dogs are buried.

We could say the same thing. We've had 35 so far, right?

If only I could whistle and all the dogs we've ever had would come running.

The boys found the tracks. Clearly defined in the furrows of the plot at the back. Come and look at this! Deep or faint. And all the stems, severed by sharp – filed? – teeth, a savage pruning. It wasn't clear whether or not the intruder was eating what it destroyed, whether or not it was two-legged. The father thought of the fruit crates at the market, recalled the phrases printed on the sides: 'Hernández & Sons', 'Salomón & María', 'Río Blanco'. He said to himself, I'll transport the crop to a safe place in a big crate called… Well, I can choose the name later. He told his wife the plan, I hope it works, she said, thinking: Every rescue is also designed to fail. The boys were forbidden from bringing friends home. None of their neighbours would be welcome.

The father established nightly patrols. Did the attacker sleep during the night? The goats chattered away at all hours in their pens, muttering their old biddy prayers. Without leaving the house, each family member had to take turns, walking from one window to another, covering the visible perimeter. Outside, the dogs kept guard, and the family watched them trotting around, backs glinting. Faithful pack. They sensed things, dug in the ground, backtracked. The family rewarded them, pulling thorns from their paws.

Despite all this hard work, every morning the walls had been daubed, the trees amputated, the fruit pelted. No one had heard how the house was being damaged. Things have got so wildly out of control, thought the mother. Just a month ago (was that all?) she had stood laughing in front of a fur shop window: 'Want to shed your old fur here? Trade it in for another'. No thanks!

The mannequin was wearing an unbuttoned, floor-length coat; whiteness and thickness of albino fox fur. Delving into this memory now was no comfort. It's only fruit, but. This *but* bounced keenly around her thoughts. She didn't understand, hated not understanding.

How to imagine an ideal body, how many shards make one up? Delving deep into the teachings of cryptozoology, the family invented a name for a beast. Naming is soothing.

The exterior walls of the house, painted with the juiciest papayas, chirimoyas, avocados, lucumas, hurled at a point of considerable ripeness, soursops, passion fruits, Burgundy grapes. Like coloured balls shot with compressed air, they slid down the walls until they disintegrated. On the ground the stones and seeds glowed sepia by the fruits' burst flesh.

Shall we fence off the moringa tree? the mother asked. Of the ten stems the father had smuggled back from India on a long-ago trip, one had struck. Fortified with fertiliser, its leaves protected by similar quantities of drinking water and oxygenated water, it took root. If it finds out that every part of the moringa is edible, it'll pull it up by the roots and throw it in our faces, the father said. He valued this particular tree, getting it ready for a future of scarcity, of crises. They had a cherry tree from Surinam, too.

Like the dogs, the children found fumbling clues. When they were little, they made friends on the beach. They would bury other children's toys – little plastic figures with their battle gear or briefcases; not tanning any longer, their owners would swap them for war, chucking sand into each other's eyes. The brothers looked closely, hands like spades – when would the plastic bodies resurface? Every childish object is a treasure to be lost. They dug up intact figures, a leg, an arm. And if all they recovered were little mutilated figures, they'd throw them away without ever stopping to wonder why they couldn't worship them. And who had registered these incidents? No one. Not their parents, not the other children, not the parents of those children, not the lifeguard from his hut, not the nearby towel-dwellers. A brother is a witness. In the summer, which progressed motionless or in great leaps, they found it easy to throw themselves into this singular game, to keep themselves busy, to attack, to brag. To be discreet about their forgeries.

The youngest said to the oldest: Remember the ant lions?

No.

We discovered them because we saw craters in the sand in the park. We scooped two up and put them in an empty matchbox – remember now?

Oh yeah: we put some sand in with them and everything, and one of them ate the other one. I couldn't believe it.

Me neither. You know what? The one that died was the ant, the lion survived.

Yeah, it feels like a million years ago. I was ten and you were eight.

The brothers looked at each other and fell silent, as if talking too much would shatter an epiphany that could last them their whole lives.

Just as in the past they had come together to bury other people's belongings, now they rehearsed a strategy for revealing the incident: This has got too much for us now, said one brother; this animal, or whatever it is, goes beyond all logic, it's absurd. They decided to get in touch with their old university, ask for expert help. They explained the raids in detail, the fruit-attacks, day after day, the fearsome and formidable cunning, the escalation, its cadence, the feeling of being watched.

This affects us. We're certain it isn't anyone in the family.

As my brother says, we have no motive.

They appealed to the academics with a question: Can you imagine the publications you could be part of?

They were promised a veterinarian, a palaeontologist, a forensic anthropologist and a geneticist.

One night, before going to sleep:

The mother: Look me in the eyes – are you the one doing this?

The father: Of course not. Why would I do that? I don't understand it either. I don't want it to drive me crazy.

She: It's fruit, for now, but if it's something else later on, something worse, will you be able to protect us?

He: I don't know. I imagine it'll become clear, I don't know.

She: I'm scared of becoming like my aunt Queta. First she was afraid of confined spaces, and then of open spaces.

In the week of fieldwork, of collecting samples, the attacker vanished with the tact of someone who knows not to outstay their welcome. No prints, no fruit. Like an abstract expressionist mural, the outside of the house was striking for a certain harmony between the drip painting technique and the use of colour. Anyone might have said: It's not just fruit, it's art.

The experts: The biological evidence may be contaminated by human pathogens. Faecal deposits. From the dogs, for instance, that's right. But we mustn't get ahead of ourselves or we'll fall prey to conjecture.

They counted their instruments. They laid them out ostentatiously. The father thought: They're exaggerating. They authorised the family to observe their work on the condition that they stayed inside the house. The house, like a function room for hire with its sign: 'Dance floor not to be viewed while a party is under way.'

They ate tinned food or three-minute soups. The provisions from a strictly planned-out apocalyptic larder, like in a nuclear summer.

Sitting at the table, the youngest son: The good side to all this is that they believed us. The fact that they're here is a victory.

This said, he asked his mother for a hug. She, sitting next to him, embraced him, kissed his forehead and whispered animistic lines to him until he was lulled to sleep.

I dreamed all kinds of things, he said afterwards.

What did you dream? the father asked.

His son looked at him with tired eyes, eyes returned from a deep sleep. He didn't want to talk. He had woken up with a simple word on his lips: home. And had found a new meaning for it: where the hunts take place.

Each one of them came up with their own forms of entertainment, their own routine. They accepted life like a play inside a zoo. Let's imagine we're on holiday at an all-inclusive hotel, the father kept saying.

The mother was struck by the story of a family that had lived a quadrupedal life. In a documentary they were being shown how to walk upright. No, they said to everything: No! The director wondered aloud if the first word pronounced by humans was 'no'. From the cave-house, he plotted the profits of all things uncivilised. The documentary was a success.

The youngest son shut himself up in the bathroom. Nobody protested. He practised making faces in front of the mirror, the whole gamut from shock to terror. He opened his eyes and stretched his mouth open wide until it hurt. Is this what fear would be like? If someone saw me grimacing in the bathroom they could say: It's you, it was you all along. He thought about the ant lion he had led to its death as a boy and understood, with irritated surprise, that he had left childhood behind a long time ago, that he was alone. If only we could hide in an attic and come out once the conflict was over; why does this have to happen now, and why to us?

The older son had been hounded by a night terror in primary school. Like an interrupted dream that resurfaces hundreds of nights later and continues, the memory came back to life. He was in the family smallholding, standing by a scarecrow. Someone was inhabiting it and held his gaze. A singular invention, the scarecrow. Its spine is a broom. Dress it in your own trousers and shirt, stitch a crimson curve for its mouth, stick it in the ground, set it up, all smiles, amid the loneliness of the crickets. In order to scare, first attract. In its eyes lies the truth. The older son is suspicious – still – of the scarecrows on whose arms crows come to roost; what if someone thinks that the man in the scarecrow is me?

The father watched things unfold in his domain. He hummed to himself. Oh, the refrains he would whistle, with delicious emphasis! How long are they going to keep us waiting here? Did I water the plants properly? The cherry tree from Surinam! He had forgotten to prune it, yet again. Its branches were forever bent from the dead weight of withered twigs. To nourish a waste so persistently – a carelessness for which he forgave himself at once. He thought too of the goats consuming the fodder at their leisure. And of the dogs, waiting for them, missing them. Of his sons domesticating themselves for life. The house had become an embassy, a dangerous country, a border, an exclusion zone. They would leave when they were granted permission. Absolved, thought the father, when we're absolved. He watched the collecting and the sniffing, the filling in of forms, the chiaroscuro details that the experts slowly circled, lining up to scrutinise the walls. The songs quivered in his mind, like hakas. Dalida and Alain Delon. Romina and Albano. And once more he thought, when I die, the thing I'll miss the most won't be food, it will be music. Being a little bit scared is doing us good; soon we'll have an answer, expected or incredible; we will learn.

But something interrupted his ramblings.

The anthropologist pushed the geneticist against one of the fruit-spattered walls. Her pipette fell to the floor and smashed. She turned towards the anthropologist to complain. A stain on her nose. They laughed, laughed a lot, kissed each other.

The father: Look at them, mocking us, and on our territory!

No one heard him. The mother was reading in the dining room, the eldest son was napping in his room and the youngest was making faces in front of the bathroom mirror.

The palaeontologist looked over at the house. Towards the concerned shadow in the window. Ha! Families are a Lazarus taxon, they never go extinct, he thought (it was a smile for himself, not the world), and carried on working.

The beloved plot of land, barely a hectare, preserved from generation to generation, ended up open like an orographic study, an archaeological site, a tomb.

Before they left, the team of experts spoke: We'll give you our assessment in due course.

When is 'in due course'? asked the eldest son.

As soon as possible.

The attacks returned.

More fruit smashed against the walls. Jam tumbling chaotically down. How to find a single blank space, a liberating one, lost familiarity? The pips all splattered, threatening, like loose roller-skate wheels, nails on the road. It stank.

On the first evening they all ate together since the visit, the father paused before venturing: When your mother and I bought this table, we chose a round one so we could all look each other in the eye, so I'm going to say it. It's as if the house itself were rotting.

A different action. One by one, the tiles were stripped from their tightly packed arrangement and sent into the front garden, down onto the gravel path. Tiles in their brickish shade of abandonment, all over the place. A calculated aggression without victims. The sun devoured them, like hollowed-out tortoise shells lying belly-up. Shorn of its characteristic decoration, the roof of the house heralded another disintegration; a dome was losing its segments.

What would it start throwing next – branches, animals? Everything urged the eyes upward: astonishment at this glorious moment, like the compulsion to gaze into an eclipse. But the family would walk in without noticing the exposed beams. Within the long shot, a flipped medium shot; instead of cutting out the legs, cutting off the head.

The most intimate space violated, the house.

If we'd had a weathervane, it would have ripped it off by now, said the mother. She suspected that some things were impossible to measure. Bewilderment, for example.

We would have lost all sense of direction, the youngest son said.

We already have, it's happening now, said the eldest. What shall we do?

And the father: It's taken a major step, so I'm going to take another one. I'll get hold of a pressure washer and we're going to leave those walls spotless – so clean we'll be able to see the first layer of skin. Who's going to help me? It's a lot of work.

We'll take it in turns, the boys promised.

Good, said the mother.

If it was tightrope walking across the roof tiles and destroying them, it was looking for something. No longer should it bear a harmless nickname, still less a pet's. They went to sleep afraid; to dream is to think. The brothers stopped drinking water after six in the evening. Neither of them wanted to have to get up in the night to go to the toilet. The dogs, tired and listless. The children wanted to let them sleep in the house for the first time. Or in the shed, even. No. The father would rather they didn't get into bad habits. The dogs are getting depressed too, the mother said to the boys; to the father: They've given up. The two largest and youngest, curled up in the same little cubbyhole, muzzles touching, like never before: a broken drawer from the chest inherited from the children's paternal grandmother, lined with old sheets the boys took from their own beds. The other dogs slept pressed up against the windows of the main bedroom. Their heads twitched without their eyelids opening.

In the early hours of the morning they were awoken by barking, a painful thump. A fall from roof to ground. The mother leaped out of bed and they all followed after her.

Blood ran from where they stood as far as the chest of drawers.

In the midst of the ecstatic, growling dogs, damp from this impromptu hunt, a bulky shape lay slowly cooling.

7.

THIS IS THE MAN

I was six years old.

My father left us when I was born. I've never met him or felt obliged to go looking for him. He disappeared from our lives, I killed him in my head. Who wants to go looking for someone who doesn't hope to be found? How do you converse with someone who isn't there? I'd like to make up a story for myself like this one:

One day after my nineteenth birthday, my father walked out.
Before he left, he gave me a box of shirts and books, saying:
Everything you need to know about life is here.

My mother would leave me at my grandmother's house in the afternoons; after lunch, she'd go back to work. Her parents' house was three blocks from our apartment. On the first floor lived my aunt and uncle, my mother's sister and her husband. With a private entrance. You never even knew if they were home or not. They have a son. Sandro. He's four years older than me. I remember the first time we played together. To be friends, much more than first cousins; to be brothers. I'd found a companion.

By then my mother had noticed I was crazy about bright colours. She would send me over to my grandmother's house armed with watercolours, paints, crayons and craft paper to share with Sandro. He loved drawing with me. I taught him to forget about tracing, how to make his own marks. Sandro was no good at colouring in. He would grow tired, start to make boats out of the paper. More and more boats. Different sizes. He was very good at that.

My aunt and uncle worked; my grandmother looked after us. She had been an old lady forever. She spent the day playing patience on top of my aunt and uncle's piano. They had inherited that piano, and they always said: It's staying here because one day Sandro will have lessons. Their favourite saying: 'One day'. They never did hire a teacher. Perhaps I would have benefited with these great big hands. If only I'd been a pianist and not a painter.

We amused ourselves watching our grandmother. All her funny habits. Boiling coffee with an onion. Sweeping the kitchen until the broom became her new walking stick. Wrapping up each and every fragment like an important little kernel, brooches, buttons, badges, passports, lockets, stowing them away in her bedside table. Praying to the patron saint of lost objects. Grandmother was patient and showed us how to order the aces and the kings from each suit, and we learned as quickly as we grew bored. She would send us off to paint in the garage: Now clear off, you know where to go. We'd messed up the living room floor by walking all over it, she'd say. If we dawdled on our way to the garage, she would point her walking stick at us, half joking, half serious. That living room floor. No one could scuff it. It was parquet, meticulously clean and gleaming. Lacquer.

The garage was a covered one. Neither my aunt and uncle nor my grandmother had a car. On one of the walls was a tap that dripped constantly. Relentlessly. It dripped and dripped, that tap, as if the cement floor were thirsty. Mum would always say: Leaving taps dripping on purpose is a selfish act, especially when I left the tap running while brushing my teeth, because half the world was thirsty. She would say, quoting a writer: When you're thirsty you say that you could drink up all the water in an oasis, but it doesn't matter how thirsty you are, you'd only be able to drink three glasses in a row because of physics. I was slowly learning that Grandmother was selfish.

These are my things. Out to the garage with you.

Grandmother's voice had a punishing intent. Sandro and I found the idea of having our own den very satisfying. Two little boys can make a fortress for themselves with four chairs. We had a four-by-four space to enjoy at our leisure. One of the garage's doors led straight into the kitchen; the other was the huge one that opened onto the street. Grandmother had forbidden us to close this first door; she wanted to hear us playing. She was very deaf. Almost completely deaf. Hear us playing – what a joke! I wished I had enough money to buy her the hearing aid on the advert on the telly. A pin dropped in a dining room and a voiceover asked an old man: Can you hear that? and from his bedroom he replied: Loud and clear. It seemed as if Grandmother never understood, as if she was always the one speaking. And she spoke very little, just enough to hoard indifference and complaints. She popped her head in a few times. Twice her walking stick appeared round the door, and she ventured in and asked us to show her our cheeks so she could kiss them. So strange. I wiped my face with my hand several times. Grandmother smelled of a mixture of talcum powder and old cologne – 'widow's perfume', my mother called it – and had tough black hairs growing out of her face that prickled you (she kept an electric razor on top of the toilet). It drove me mad that she did nothing about the dripping tap. Grandmother? Nothing. Although we did grow used to it very quickly, as if it were a third companion. The garage stank of centuries of damp, of catacomb. Do you remember that smell, did you ever do a school trip to an old church? Two solitary little boys. Alone. Sandro copied my drawings and worked hard at his little boats.

I kept my drawings to show them to my mother later. She always came home exhausted, but she made the effort. After all the work he'd put into them, Sandro would tear up most of his creations and throw them in the bin. Because they're all the same, he'd say; I can't make any of them look different. I stared at him uncomprehending; is he stupid or just pretending? I replied: That's because you fold them like this then like that. I laughed at him and he laughed along with me.

One of those afternoons, he asked me to turn on the tap. It was dripping every two minutes, more or less. Turn it more, he said, more! A rivulet formed that headed towards the kitchen, flooding it.

This was such an unexpected thing; exhilarating, that's what it was. The floor of the garage sloped down towards the kitchen rather than being at the same level as the house. You know what children are like. With water everything's a game, even when there's waste. All at once, the dripping tap stopped troubling me. The water was alive. Keep turning it! The change in Sandro's face, spectacular: he was the older of the two of us; the captain decided. I turned the tap as far as I could, he picked up one of his little boats and placed it in the current. We watched it move forward as if pushed by invisible winds up to the kitchen door, crashing up against it, prow crumpling like a furrowed brow.

The one thing we couldn't neglect was drying the kitchen floor. We knew where the mops were kept. Grandmother never had to find out. Nor did Mum. There would be no telling off. I would dry the parquet really thoroughly, Grandmother's walking stick would never slip. I didn't want to witness the horror of her falling. I was always afraid of this, that Grandmother might have a fall in my absence and that Sandro might fail to call the numbers pinned on the wall. My mother always said: I'd feel so much happier if Grandmother lived with us, but our house is about as wide as the sofa. I'd say to myself: Sandro will get muddled up and do something stupid with the telephone.

The water continued to flow, the same rushing sound. When I tried to turn off the tap, Sandro wouldn't let me. He came up to me, came up too close. He was smiling. I hesitated, wondering if he might be about to hit me. Why would he improvise now? Sandro was unimaginative in his games, in everything. He put his mouth close to my ear and said: Pull down your trousers. It was a request. In no way was it an order.

What for, Sandro? What's up?

Just do it.

The same soft voice, but his ten-year-old face had hardened; it looked like that of an adult, my uncle's face. He pushed me and I fell to the floor. I tried to get up. Each time, I slipped in the water, then slipped again. Sandro knelt down beside me and removed my shoes with care, tenderly, like the older brother who lovingly helps to undress his ill brother and put him to bed. With the same patience he removed my trousers. No, he did not look me in the eyes. Was there compassion in them, or were they simply focussing? I couldn't tell if he was going to hurt me or not. How could I know? He didn't behave badly and yet. I looked at the ravaged boat up against the door, then at the tap. I cried out with all my might; who was going to hear me?

For the rest of the year, Sandro did to me what he did to me in that place and nobody found out. He'd put his arms around me. He'd talk a lot, saying any old thing that came into his head. I heard only a tangle of words, I didn't want to listen; if I understood I would always understand, and I didn't want to. He'd help me pull my trousers up, I'll undress you, I'll dress you, in that vein. He'd say: Now you can turn off the tap and dry the kitchen floor, we don't want Grandmother falling over.

On the day of my seventh birthday I told my mother I was never going to Grandmother's house again. What's the matter? Is Grandmother or Sandro being mean to you? Are they hitting you? I told her that Grandmother wouldn't fix the tap in the garage. If only I had been able to show her where it hurt.

It hurt everywhere.

Mum, not understanding why a dripping tap could make me cry, blamed herself for having convinced me it was selfish to leave the water running. That year I entered the first grade and signed up for a painting class, at my own insistence. They accepted me despite my age. When I turned fifteen and got my first girlfriend, I told Mum what had happened. Earlier that night she had said to me: I'm more exhausted than ever today. Really shattered. I thought, she's so tired that if I talk now, she'll have to listen.

At family parties, Sandro would get drunk. Everyone allowed it. Grandmother had died by this point. No one noticed me coping with the threat. Sandro managed to corner me, whispering into my ear in a friendly voice: Your mum is an idiot. Doesn't she realise you look like a poof with those salmon-coloured trousers on? I suppose if someone had seen us from a distance, they would have shouted for everyone to come and see the older cousin swaggering around in front of the younger: Come on, just fight why don't you, have at each other like bulls or cocks. You're at that age – you're men now. I felt like I'd been thrown out of the party. I despised my salmon-coloured trousers. I didn't struggle. Sandro was two heads taller than me. He'd had a massive growth spurt. I was afraid of him. Of the evil king, the lifelong damage. The dread before sleep. The terror of someone forced to walk into the sea without knowing how to swim, and who fears drowning in the shallows, without the relief of breaking through the wave that swallows him up. Sandro knew what I was thinking: I would be the poof, not him. I, the skinny little runt, the introvert, the one with the hands that were disproportionately large compared to the rest of my body, the 'painter in the family'.

Holding back her tears (she was trying so hard not to cry!), Mum said, Don't ever tell a girl this, or she won't want to be with you. They'll think you're a poof. And you're not a poof. You're my son. The only poof is that son of a bitch Sandro. I'd strangle him myself if I could.

Adulthood is an artificial beach the mind prolongs. This is why, when I paint Sandro, I paint him as a child, at the same age. If I were to paint him as an adult, I would hate him.

My mother fell silent: Family is family, she said.

Revenge roams around for a while, running deep, then forgets about retribution. Having done everything for me; having done nothing at the same time. There is shadow, and there is light.

My mother died two weeks ago; she said to me: If I made a mistake it was an oversight. Forgive me, as I've forgiven you.

I said to her: I don't forgive you, and I don't plan on forgiving you ever.

And I sprayed her with her favourite cologne.

Aside from her, I haven't told anyone else what I've told you.

It's good for me to talk to a woman, to tell her, this is the man I am, this is the man.

8.

WE, THE SHIPWRECKED

My father and I have become guerrillas.
The hospital, an island.
I shout to him: Come on, comrade, we've got to keep on fighting until the end.
Apart from his beard and all the excitement there is nothing revolutionary about our dream.

★ ★ ★

I persist on the side of the living while my father lists his wishes, which grow smaller and more ridiculous.

He grows irritated, glances towards the window, says: Now clear off.

I go back home.
The city breathes silence.
Just one dog. Mine.
The plants sprinkling each other from their pots.
Everything I love is still alive.

My father's anger infuriates me, and I take solace in being able to hate him.

His phrases peppered with:
I never
I would have
I ought to have
If only I
My reply: my silence.

In the ambulance he asks to be put in facing the door.
You always go in facing the door, they tell him.
His free arm points:
I took a walk there with your mother once.
My tailor used to live there.
My dentist was over there.
We used to go there to eat pasta.
This is where you lent me your bike.
The city says goodbye to him: He was here.

He was a little boy, too – chasing after a lizard, clutching a stone and a spinning top – and wavered at which to throw first.
An idea of childhood: this is what I inherit from my father.

He calls me.
He takes me by the arm as he speaks, doesn't let go. His hand, once a claw, a compress, a tourniquet; now, just a hand. The same size as mine.
A pianist's hands.
A sculptor's hands
A basketball player's hands.
Hands for smacking.
This is what his hands used to say.

This is what my own say now.

He feeds himself with both hands, one mouthful after another, with the greed of someone recovering the pleasure of flavours long-dead.

His legs are paralysed. One of them lifts up by reflex. It's levitating, he says.

I tell him that a woman asked to share my table in the cafeteria. All the other tables were occupied.
What was she like?
About your age. Grey hair. Good-looking. A low voice.
And what did she say to you?
She said: I'm God. I thought, she's mad. Who knows what kind of look I gave her. She explained: I'm an air traffic controller.
Ah, so this is why you're late? Because you were having breakfast with God?

One evening he remembers: When you were a little girl you said, 'If I die one day…,' And I corrected you: 'You are going to die one day, you and all of us, and that's why we say "when I die".'

My father is banned from getting the newspaper. I take them to him camouflaged in a bag of toilet roll. He secretly cuts out headlines and saves them. He's had this habit for some time. The hospital won't give him scissors; he uses his fingers. His scraps, their edges uneven, the odd missing letter which we fill in. He hides them in cartons of pills. He shows me his life summary, his own personal news bulletin, his hospital headlines:
IF YOU WERE A SCIENCE, WHICH ONE WOULD YOU BE?

SLEW OF ICEBERGS
A SYSTEM FOR DETECTING GLUCOSE IN DIABETICS' TEARS
VERSE IS NEVER FREE
RUNNING FOR 40 YEARS EXTENDS YOUR LIFE BY 3
WHY DOES IT RAIN FISH?
He says: It's a good thing I didn't take out a subscription to the paper this year.

Mourning begins before death. I run in mourning and the shadow of my own death comes after me. I'm certain I'll die from the same illness, the same year as my father. I want X-rays and scans, to see inside myself, osseous and soft, my stomach, my arteries, the soles of my feet and my birth marks, each and every hair follicle.
Then this thought will reverse. I'll take it back. I'll live with my eyes in suspense.

My father: El Silencio and Los Órganos. You realise your favourite beaches are both musical?

I remember.

I've promised my father one more summer.

* * *

I cried to my father in his casket.
I tied a handkerchief around his head. To preserve his dentures under the moustache he tended so meticulously. The funeral parlour erased that gesture. In its place: a smile of chilled cotton wool balls and a violet-coloured rose on his shirt (I'd crossed his hands over his chest. His veins were still warm and blue).

My mother said: I'll go to the wake first and decorate everything.
Making it all nice, red roses and my mother's message on top of the coffin: Your wife, who always loved you.
My father had told me: If there is a hell, I've already been through it with your mother.
Never do flowers reek with such violence as at a wake.
Someone pipes down: It smells of death.
Someone else: If you're not taking them all to the cemetery, can I take a bunch home?
On a Tears-of-Christ (a redundant name for mortuary flowers), the legend: Your malaria friends.
My sister's biologist colleagues and their lacerating laughter, like a sickness.

* * *

I dress my father in the suit he'd had made for my sister's wedding.
Mum said: No shirt, that doesn't matter, put the jacket straight onto his bare skin, no one will notice.
I put an old shirt on him, an un-ironed one. The nurse helped me in case rigor mortis set in.
Mum was a shout with a cigarette. Later, a voice in the doorway.
Dad had spent the last two weeks at my house, in the middle of the living room; he had no underpants, only a dressing gown.
Without thinking, I took a pair of my knickers from the drawer.
I dressed him in the jacket, his grey trousers, his socks.
He looked as good as a dead man ready for a wedding can look.
The voice in the doorway shouted: Don't put shoes on him, it's bad luck. And you – put on some red knickers to

mark the end of the mourning period.
I kept the promise I made to Dad: not to shave off his moustache.
We never spoke about the underwear.

* * *

I still haven't taken care of Dad's ashes.
When he was alive he hated his ashes, the ones from his cigarettes.
What would he have done with my dead body?
He would have gathered all the ashes together: You and my cigarettes are the things I love the most.
He tried to stop smoking for me.
I tried to start for him.
Look, he said, from his hospital bed: The ceiling over there, those lights, they look like New York, don't they?
In Times Square, 1951, my father smoked a cigarette.
This is documented in a photograph inside a suitcase I can no longer open.

* * *

Soon it will be beach season.
One more summer, I promised my father.
When I throw his ashes to the winds: Will his body shape itself again upon the sand?
Will I close his eyes once more to protect them from the light?

9.

LOVEBIRD

The most unforgettable day in the neighbourhood, Mrs Queta says. When Luisa and her family moved in. She was impressed: Luisa stopped traffic; she stopped everything. She would be a distinguished addition. Distinction was something necessary, it was lacking, that much was *e-vi-dent*. She couldn't be the only one annoyed by it: fruit and vegetable sellers, scrap metal collectors hawking their services: *Catreee,* an old term for a camp bed, *catreee… any old rag and booone*, oh yes indeed, such a grating, nasal tone. She wanted to ring her husband at work, tell him about it right away. He had told her: You're only to interrupt me again if it's very important.

This *was* important. Very. She would start by piquing his interest. She had a real talent for this: You should see this new woman who's just moved in next door!

He would guess she was an ex-prisoner, a murderess. Something like that. She would go on about Luisa's great beauty and he would be able to imagine her before his own experience came to fruition. She knew what her husband was like – not for nothing had they been married for twenty years, with all the pros and cons entailed by such a feat. Women like Luisa, especially in magazines, with contradictory captions such as: Sweet & Flirty. She would go and introduce herself. The urge to be the first, the first at everything. Luisa looked intelligent. Eyes of an adventurous cat. Mrs Queta counted two hours after the removal van drove away. She watched keenly through the living room window, waiting for an opportune moment. Since no moment is opportune, she went and rang the bell. Nothing glimpseable through the curtains. Luisa herself opened the door. She, in all her splendour. Mrs Queta stammered internally.

Hello, she clucked, I'm your neighbour. She had lost patience with herself.

I saw you this morning. What's up?

What's your name?

Was that it? Would she just say Luisa? What about her surname? And those great big eyes?

Did you know your name means 'warrior'?

Don't remind me – I'm so tired of fighting all the time.

She sought to match this answer, to come back with an equally dramatic reply. Over the years she'd learned to hold back a little: Of course, Luisa. Even though our mothers spent nine months thinking up the right name for us, it's best not to think too hard about it.

And yours?

Enriqueta. Humiliated by her short nickname, Mrs Queta thought she'd been standing in the doorway long enough, and awkwardly waved four fingers – a little girl saying goodbye to her cartoons, 'Say bye-bye to the birdie, darling!'

Next time she would come prepared; Luisa wouldn't catch her off guard. The Warrior. She decided to hold off calling her husband. He would meet their new neighbour eventually. Oh yes indeed. This thought assuaged her anxiety. For a time.

The next encounter took place in the bakery. Mrs Queta found Luisa looking at the bread. Eyes of a curious cat.

I recommend the French stick, it's lovely and crusty, Queta murmured into her neighbour's ear. A little girl in her class at primary school used to give her the answers to exam questions like this, the wrong answers.

Luisa gave a start. I'm after empanadas.

Empanadas? Ah, but they only do chicken ones here, and they're drier than the road out south in the summer. Mrs Queta focussed her mind. Of course – it must be one of those decisive moments when Luisa lived up to her name: choosing empanadas could be a titanic battle, why not? Choosing is harder than being chosen. Mrs Queta found everyday routine painful too, especially the gondola of detergents at the supermarket. So overwhelming! Some had little blue and white grains in, others blue and green ones, still others blue and red. Before, you would wash clothes with the same soap you used to boil up tea towels and nappies. Now, soap powder for washing clothes and soap for washing your body both contain brightly coloured little granules. And the display racks in supermarkets are called 'gondolas.' And what the hell did Venice have to do with a supermarket? Ah, right, Luisa said.

Mrs Queta had hoped for much more from Luisa's family.

To choose a dull moustachioed man as a husband, with her being how she was, so very, very… *that*. Mrs Queta found moustaches repulsive. The kids weren't all bad, although they did blast the afternoons with their flute playing. They looked like miniature adults with excess baggage, lugging around backpacks in which trainers, thermoses, half-eaten sandwiches, extracurricular activities could be glimpsed. Luisa's children might be like adults, loveable and detestable. Depending on what? Well, lots of things.

Mrs Queta confided in her husband (he was yet to meet Luisa, and had only seen the children head off to their lessons, waving at their little friends): Those kids don't go to school, they go to a conservatoire for deaf children.

Her husband would lock himself in the bathroom to play Tetris, the little blocks shifting up-and-down on his phone. Avoiding his wife's verbal diarrhoea. Whenever she shouted, he replied: I'm comiiing! He wasn't coming. So manifestly was he not coming that Queta's foot would kick at the door, and he would emerge, the face of a man struck down by diarrhoea and she, twisting her face into pity, amused by this attack of stomach flu. Until one day, it dawned on her husband: Queta is just like a Tetris block. Even she doesn't know where she fits, and, when she does fit somewhere, when is the game over and why? And he loved her, because in this life one must be grateful for the choices one makes and re-makes daily, must grow accustomed to settling for a poor imitation. Now, her husband believed, the known world had been exhausted, and the world to be worshipped was happening out in the street. Observing what went on beyond the living room window, swapping places with someone else: this made Queta a desiring being. Queta, satellite and moon of the same atmospheres; her life, an old dolls house, the armchairs stacked up in obvious corners awaiting an untidy hand. As a child she would play at lying belly-down on the floor underneath the stairs and reimagining the ceiling as a space you could walk on. If she had ever walked close to a precipice, Queta, to her friend: Let's go and look over the edge, see what's going on.

The younger version of herself had loved to improvise, to mess around. Until the tree changed everything.

For instance. On their way to the beach on the old highway, her husband at the wheel, they came across a big top with a mouldering awning, and she had shouted: STOP! *The International Little Dwarf Circus* had given them two-for-one entry and they managed to squeeze into the front row. Thrilled by the aerial somersaults to come, she gazed up at the ceiling to see if she could make out any swings, strips of fabric, trapezes, ladders, a net. The ceiling was the underside of the tent, nothing more. To kill time, she told her husband that soon they would hear: Break a leg! They only say that in the theatre, her husband corrected her. She was about to challenge him on this when out came the clown in his ridiculous attire. The first act always belongs to the clown, he'll announce the fun in two halves, ask for applause for the children, promise things never seen before. They didn't see any children, just adults munching popcorn and swigging beer straight from the bottle. They shifted in their seats.

The clown said: Direct from Monte Carlo, just what you've all been waiting for, The Fantastic Siracusa Brothers! At this point, her husband said: I was at school with a Juana Siracusa, we used to say 'Juanita Siracusa, loose little boozer.' Mrs Queta immediately asked him if he had had a thing with her.

Four dwarves with toned bodies and tight clothing entered, two men and two women, their sizes as varied as the toes on a foot. One of them shouted, Hup! and the rest of them all climbed swiftly on top of each other, completely in synch. The lights silhouetted the balance, four mouths smiling as one. The little pink and blue costumes glittered with sequins. Down, one shouted, and they all leapt off perfectly, one after the other, domino-style. Hup! but with a different inflection, and from the back of the stage out trotted the most disturbing component, a dwarf dog, curly-haired and wearing a little pair of neon green trainers. Hup! and the fluffy little thing went stock still, like a spoiled lapdog, out of practice and out of prizes; it sniffed the air lazily with an expression that said *I want out of here*. The dwarves that had disappeared now returned with a big builder's ladder. They arranged themselves side by side in a line and to the cry of Up we go! deftly lifted the ladder up onto their shoulders. Hup! said one, the little dog dashing around, dodging and jumping over everything and everyone, landing on top of the ladder, four paws, four steps, flapping its propellertail. Oh, how they laughed! Mrs Queta and her husband, unprejudiced about the sizes and potential capabilities of each and every one. They set off for the beach again, all fired up, chatting excitedly about getting a dog. Neither of them had had a dog as a child, maybe it was a good idea.

Mrs Queta said: For the first few days puppies have to sleep close to their owner's slippers, so it can sleep near yours, since they smell much worse than mine.

Her husband: No. They sleep by an alarm clock, and the tick-tock reminds them of the rhythm of their mother's heart. Then he had a thought: How come we know so much about dogs if we've never had one? I'd only agree to a Dogo Argentino.

They're really big – too big, she said.

Well, that's the end of that good idea, then.

Back on the highway, Mrs Queta whispered: When we walked out, all that was left in the circus were sad clowns and animal shit.

What?

Nothing.

I thought I heard you say something.

You thought you did.

Luisa would leave for work – where? – at the same time every day, walk to the bus stop on the corner, hurrying along; everything suited her, even the three-quarter-length sleeves and white trousers that so few women can pull off. Mrs Queta would watch her walk to the end of the block and then, when she lost sight of her, would crumple as if the world itself had come crashing down.

Mrs Queta carried her sadnesses around like a bag she took with her everywhere. She called this bag 'personal effects'. Her father had committed suicide two months after her mother died. He had hung himself from the only tree in their garden. Anticipating the visit his daughter paid him every Tuesday, he had written in pencil on the wall in the hallway:

Quetita. Don't go in the back.

She didn't read it, went on through to the kitchen and looked out of the window: her father, the branch, death.

He had got everything ready, dressed in a suit and tie from previous bereavements, left cards for each child, each grandchild, and the house to a first cousin who was living hand to mouth. An envelope containing the costs of the burial and an old receipt for the grave he had paid for in the niche above his wife. He was ninety-one years old. The relatives passed from the wildest panic to bewilderment to the useless indulgence of understanding. The old man had killed himself as suspected criminals used to be hung, his gesture a tribute to the past. At the wake no one saw the joke. They didn't forgive him, nor did they judge him out loud.

If I speak of this, thought Mrs Queta, I won't ever stop crying and it's one's duty to live.

The tree changed everything.

She had become a blurred presence in the window, welcoming or bidding farewell, dissatisfied by the short-circuit between expectation and reality or resistance. The job of being alive in repetitions. As a father carefully watches his daughter's bed to make sure that her chest has stopped wheezing – that now it's just rising and falling, rising and falling – her husband reassured himself: Queta is at her imaginary balcony. He saw how her eyes were still fixed outward, a far-off look in them.

One night he would come out of his bathroom refuge without being called, would say to her, perhaps without breaking down (he would know when it happened): We have wasted our lives.

Mrs Queta would not give up.

She planned to get an animal to brighten up Luisa's life and, by extension, that of her whole family. Is it or is it not true that the best imaginary friend is an imagined animal? She hunted in pet shops; nothing very promising. Dogs, cats – nope, too much trouble. What's more, cats: toxoplasmosis; dogs: scabies. A woman's got enough on her plate what with dust mites. How can anyone get up to greet the new day knowing that those little insects eat what we shed of our skin? A hamster? No, because of rabies, and because they run around in their little wheels for no apparent reason. No way would she look after one of those. Everybody should take care of his or her own creatures. Like an unexpected revelation after watching a film, she realised instinctively what she should buy. A bird with a cage, feeder, seed, a water bottle – a complete kit, impossible to turn down, because one only turns down what is incomplete. A little bird, a morning bird. It could even come with a name. And one that produced sounds and silences more curious than those of any flute.

A musical blessing and a natural solution for both parties. Mrs Queta suddenly felt very eco-friendly. Without any guilt at the exorbitant investment – 'Give me a male so it sings nicely' – she purchased a lovebird. Of this action she confided not a peep to her husband; it was her little secret. She walked home proudly, holding the cage like a falcon trainer.

It was early afternoon.

She rang the bell.

Luisa opened the door.

The same bedazzlement. Instead of speaking, Mrs Queta held up the cage with all it contained.

What's this? Luisa the Warrior's foot wedged hard into the doorframe.

For you. For your family.

In case Luisa said nothing, Mrs Queta pushed on: To brighten up your lives. No house is complete without a little animal. They're antidotes to depression. The everyday, you know.

Don't give me that, Queta, you don't have pets in your house.

Well, sometimes my husband is a bit like... No smile attended this little joke.

Well?

I wanted to give you a housewarming present, you seem like a lovely person.

Queta, I've been living here for three months. I know the area well. And most of my neighbours, including the ones who spy on me.

Since Luisa wasn't moving her foot from the doorway, warning of growing tension, Mrs Queta said: Perhaps you don't like it? Would you rather I kept it?

I would. Those creatures should live in pairs, they die when they're on their own. They don't like solitude.

But if I keep it, my husband...

The bird flitted about in its cage, its eyes fixed longingly on the street.

It gives me no pleasure to say this, and I don't mean to sound ungrateful, but I didn't ask you for it.

There are too many negatives in that sentence, Luisa. It was simply a nice neighbourly gesture on my part; I wanted to do something for you, something lovely.

What do you want me to say? Her alley-cat eyes, humiliating Mrs Queta.

I wouldn't know what to call it. And now I'll have to buy another one. It'll finish me off twice over.

Ha, ha, well it's up to you. Goodbye. The door closing, no kiss, no 'see you'. And she found goodbyes so difficult. It all seemed to last no time at all.

How does one return a bird to a pet shop? Mrs Queta considered her options: whether she could give it to another neighbour, whether her husband would throw her out like her father did with the cat that climbed the family tree, whether it was true that – in order to survive – there should be two of the caged things. She also thought of take-off, of landing, and associated them with her favourite words: commotion, foliage, airfield, linnet, starling, lark.

Reaching her house, she turned around, stared up for a moment at the deep sky that mobilises and intimidates. Click. Go-on-fly-away. She knew then that she had risked something, Enriqueta.

Up there, higher and higher, it flew over her, and she called it by its name, wings made bold by the wind.

10.

THE HAMBERES TWINS

Better here?

Yep. I'll turn the tape recorder on. Start when it's running.

I'll just read a few sections.

OK.

It was a quiet morning, that's the first thing I can tell you. The Hamberes twins were wearing new, plain suits. They were drinking coffee out of a thermos. They pointed at the ceiling with their index fingers, and their parents and older brother said: Yes, up there. A farewell without tears or doubts.

Time?

We gave them the lethal injection at half past eleven. The twins were in adjacent beds, holding hands. They smiled at the nurses and at me. They had an identical death, just as they had envisioned. Strictly speaking, there is nothing either heroic or reprehensible in this.

We know what the course of events was. I believe it will be up to history to judge us; not now, but when the time is right.

I refused to help them, as you know. I was under constant attack; neither of them was experiencing *unendurable physical suffering caused by a serious, incurable pathological condition.*

Your colleagues refused to take part due to the absence of this requirement, seven of them confirmed to me.

Exactly. Even if congenital deafness does cause a profound and irreversible melancholy, there was no way we could consider it sufficient reason.

When did you decide to help them?

The twins returned to my consulting room accompanied by their parents and their older brother. What do they expect me to do? I thought, I had already given them a firm answer. The family told me they had been in disagreement about the twins' pact. They had tried to dissuade them, always in vain. I quote the older brother: 'They have lived together since they were eighteen years old; they're forty-five now. Three months ago, a degenerative disorder was detected which would have left them blind. They do everything together: cooking, cleaning, shopping. They're both cobblers. They would have to go into sheltered housing and depend on other people. The floor of their apartment is so clean you could eat off it.'

And what were the brothers doing while all this was being said?

Following the movement of people's lips, nodding their heads; they constantly communicated in sign language. And this is what's unusual: it wasn't any of the known sign systems.

They had a singular language.

Singular and secret. And there was something childlike in both of them, apart from the lack of scars on their eyebrows or chins, and their intelligent eyes. They had oily, shiny faces.

Was it easy to tell them apart?

I couldn't tell you with any certainty which one was

which. Each looked like the self-portrait of the other. I had to ask them: Are you Mikel, or Jordy? It was easy to imagine what they were like as children, choosing the same clothes, the same toys. Their father told me that they had gone to the consulting rooms of six different ophthalmologists to confirm the diagnosis of blindness; all of them promised palliative care. He also said: You know very well what this means. Psychiatrists prescribed them psychotropic drugs to alleviate their distress.

Let's speak about the mother now. Very few people understand her 'sacrifice', shall we say.

We can hear her in her own words: 'A mother will never accept the fact that her children want to die, but if she stops blaming herself, she will be able to understand the pain they feel. Such is a mother's love.' I searched her eyes for traces of a façade, of cynicism, madness. I found nothing, aside from acceptance. She continued: 'For my sons, the idea of never seeing each other again is the only unbearable pain.' When they left, I sat there in surprise. For the next two weeks all I could think of was the twins.

The fact is that this is an inconceivable situation.

1) I would be blamed for slaughtering them even if my hands were clean. 2) The desire to die does not mean much on its own. We have all experienced it at some point. We want to know why we must live. If I have learned anything in my years as a doctor, it is that we need company to get through the most private phase of our existence.

You didn't want to take responsibility?

What are you going to do now? my colleagues asked me; millions of people around the world live every day with the same affliction, there are people who are blind and deaf, people who are mute and lame. Which is true. I had thought of this too; how could I fail to? Not for a long time had I felt so perplexed.

Had you had any similar cases?

I am responsible for the euthanasia of 234 people, the majority of them due to terminal cancer. Not a single case like this one, not one. I helped my best friend to die. I wish I could've been anywhere else. He didn't want to go, but he understood that he had to do it. Better it be you than a stranger, he said, putting my mind at rest. It was a question of friendship.

But you had no particular sympathy towards the Hamberes brothers. Let's get back to them.

The next time they came alone. I noticed how they even walked the same, their left feet dipping slightly. On their shirt pockets they were wearing stickers with their names, like first-year university students. A joke that kept us hovering above the abyss. Suicide? I asked them, and I gave them paper and pens. Mikel was the first to write his reply: 'One of us will see the other die first.' Jordy wrote: 'It would send us mad. We know what we're asking for.' The same handwriting; why was I still surprised.

What would have happened if the twins had been two blind people about to go deaf?

That's just speculation. I can't speak about what-ifs. The psychic pain they would have felt when faced with the definitive absence of the other was already incurable. They would never be able to get over it, of that I'm certain.

This death pact has ignited new controversies and reopened legal debates.

It's good to have a conversation that reveals all the doubts. We will make interesting discoveries. I came to a conclusion and I still believe in it. No one has the right to reproach anybody else, to say: your pain seems excessive to me.

Let's talk about the news report.

Yes, I was expecting that. Did you write it?

No, but let's look at the headline: 'Over 70% of people are in favour of euthanasia in minors with the ability to make conscious decisions.'

Correct. I now have every intention of observing how children manage; we'll soon discover the scope of their spirit.

Will they really be able to just let go of life so soon?

It's a mystery. So now I hope that all these misgivings fade over the next few weeks and I can get back to work.

11.

GARDENING

In his gardening journal, the man noted down the following details:

10 a.m. / Tuesday
I've planted the last pine tree beneath a very hot sun.

Sitting down in front of the spiky pine trees, he waited.

All mornings repeated themselves in the only verb it was possible to conjugate: to wait.

He would wait for his children to visit.

He was waiting for a female presence to be authorised.

He will wait for the phosphate fertiliser.

From the concrete bench, an extension of the floor, he stared at his hands, his belly, his legs, his feet, his sandals, looking for what to do next in them.

The pines persuaded him to stare at the bellies of planes.

Kaput.

He thought about sex every day. Waking up next to a woman who would look back at him. A politician's career is very demanding, he had told all his partners – all the sacrifices that have to be made. He would fall asleep with his clothes on. The roaring of a plane, the light, they hurt him in the early morning, the anxiety of a recurring dream cutting into him: there was no way out of the place he was in.

He lived in a prison only he inhabited. A maximum-security jail fifty metres square, with a yard, close to the airport. It was a sort of yard, he told himself once again. In the bedroom, two oxygen tanks loomed next to the bed. He felt towards them variants of the same aversion: who was still paying for them and what was the aim? He would never be able to masturbate while they were still there. If he forgot to zip his fly up after urinating, who would let him know? His secret obsession of wiping down the seat with toilet paper in any bathroom, public or private – what use was that now? Even his rubbish had shrunk in size.

Nights and Sundays were awful.

Kaput, if something tormented him to the point of heartburn, a habeas corpus, a candidate struck off, a colleague under investigation, his children's profligacy. He read in no particular order, finally understanding snippets from personal diaries, poems, psychoanalysis, until his mind led him back to an earlier unhappiness: the largest salt flat in the world, where each watery mirror reflected back to him his body fissured with ancient cracks like ulexite. Fragments of himself. There was no fixed point to look at, everything was overwhelming, everything raised questions, something between magnetism and revulsion.

As they walked, looking for lights in the desert night of the salt flat, his last wife had said to him: I want to break up with you.

We came all this way just for you to be honest with me?

He recalled the useless words in the dead sky, *I have no way of getting back*, the horror of being abandoned, the sway of silence. He endured heading deeper into the desert with her, the volcanoes, the fumaroles, the geysers, the baby animal scooped up by a predator as soon as it showed its head, the chatty guide who gave everything they saw an outlandish new nickname. The origin or the end of the world in the landscape of a museum that exhibited him as he inhabited it.

He and the pine trees share similar habits of decline: both are perennial beings under multiple pressures, burdened by an exhaustion that at first goes unnoticed, until they die, if another pine overshadows them, parasitizes them. At each new little branch put out, a creator's pride is triggered in him, moving him deeply; a vanity he cannot boast about, delight itself. He can feel almost content, almost grateful. Almost alive. And before? The gardens of the houses, annexes belonging to his wife, his children; he would invite himself there. The gardeners would turn up with their own junk, names forgotten as soon as uttered. If in a moment of distraction one of his feet became tangled in a hosepipe: Sack that half-wit or I'm going to injure myself! He had a horror of sending cut flowers – they were dead, what on earth was beautiful about them? The neighbours despised him. For his parties, for his neatly pruned gardens, for the long line of encroaching cars, for the shared dissatisfaction that made them equals. One neighbour brightened up – he had a dreadful idea. He placed coffins all around his courtyard to make a horrifying vista.

Then he would joke with his guests: You must forgive the neighbours' funeral parlour there; in any case, it's not an old people's home, nothing to fear.

He spoke to the police at the door. Welcoming, requesting, thanking, exchanging. They worked shifts.

What would their faces be like? Fat in the fattening stage, from eating out of sheer boredom. His lawyer was the one he saw often. An eye-wateringly expensive bore who charged him more because he appeared on TV, because he brought him books every week. He told relentless anecdotes about his achievements, starting every sentence with: 'It's an occupational hazard for me, but...' His name was Damián. Even Damián's name was suspect. He was the best.

He had dismissed the fantasy of planting monkey puzzle trees. It would take twenty-five years for *Araucaria araucana* to come up to his knees. And then there was the secondary, although not insignificant, problem of the climate. He needed evidence, branch after branch, to be able to say to himself: Today they look bigger than yesterday. He first came across them at a campsite with his children. You would look at them, even a slender, solitary one, ghostly white, as if covered in snow despite the summer, and know intuitively, this is what it means to last forever.

The pines out in the yard formed a square within a square. Spiky little stakes in progress. I'm going to watch them grow. Like my children. No: multiply *them* by zero even though I hoped for everything. A single visit, hello and goodbye, a minimal note. He wrote them letters crawling with memories. Each moment after the next. To travel, at least in the mind, to the places they explored together, to the mornings caught unawares, to the hours with most light. His children lay down on the grass watching lenticular clouds make their journey across the sky – 'You see the mushroom? And those ones that look like sand dunes? They're so pretty.' It's a waste of time inventing what isn't there, he had told them, the only truth is reality. Now he missed them frozen in childhood, couldn't think of them as adults. They ran once more down the corridors, touching the walls with their grubby hands, diving headfirst into the water – 'Look, Daddy!' – they bellyflopped, pulled at the hair on his neck while he was driving, kissed him when he got in from the office, and he would have liked to talk about this with someone, to say out loud, I remember them so clearly, I love them as they were.

He decided to paint them as they are.

He drew all three faces, including his own, reinstating his mole, his witch-like nose, everything fixed; he painted his eyes small but shrewd, that gaze he was told made him look eternally suspicious.

He sent them the painting.

He feared this nightmare: the dilated sphincters, the bedsores forming on his back, his children repulsed.

As if the time of trees were also his own, he imagined himself in prison until the pines grew up past the wall. The yard would be a yard no longer. A garden with its own ecosystems. A persistent, promising beauty. The day he arrived in prison he compared it to an empty bombed-out lot. The first few weeks the empty walls plunged him deep into a rebellious state. He wanted to go out to buy ornaments. The risk of refining that which tethers us: food, bed, worry, a dog.

Before this life, another life smiled at him when twenty prisoners escaped through a hole – the advantages of an earthquake. Many of them went home to sleep in their own beds. One of them handed himself in the next day, and the front pages led with:

GERMÁN, THE PRISONER WHO CAME BACK IN HIS PYJAMAS

That guy Germán, what a character. A free man loses the pretence of escape.

He missed the sea. He had swum among jellyfish, was spooked by their transparent souls. Even so, he thought, the sea is far more dangerous when it reaches land than out at sea.

One afternoon, ambushed by a cough, the policemen asked him, Are you alright? With an effort he replied: We are fine! Who was this 'we'?

He had been locked up for a year.

Four seasons, unmarked birthdays and anniversaries, the cautious lapse of a grief he suffered, hoarding mistakes, familiarising himself with his file (he recognised and did not recognise himself, like a madman's memory), learning from books about the silence of animals, I had to do everything myself, they'll soon come tumbling down, you can't build a house of cards with one card alone, they'll be feeling as free as a shipwrecked sailor on his imperceptible island.

He knew how to console himself. Historic leaders wrote their most important works or became statistics, being locked up either kills or revives you, it disrupts everything. Sanity, telling the difference between day and night, accepting confusion in the face of a radical experience.

And if compulsions are treasures from childhood, he was slowly losing them one by one. No longer did he frantically pat his pockets to check for loose change, car keys. What ought to have been there was no longer there. The café he went to some mornings, his name spelt wrong on the cardboard cup; one yearns to reread one's own name, even in those circumstances. Of what might surround him, the ever-stranger sound of the streets connecting the city; his beloved pine trees, everything real, tangible hope, leaves are leaves, they grow green with his touch.

It's not that he'd grown accustomed to it. He had grown unaccustomed.

He thought: Show me someone innocent, life is the most difficult journey, a single name, we determine it; the apple and the snake, if there is a god, we're already in paradise. We can feel the urge to urinate and to drink, the organs, body, desire – they all long to contradict each other.

Visitor, they shouted. It's so unreal, reckless, even, with one's expectations, an announcement like this in a prison. Visitor.

What did you say? Hang on. He stood up. He was sweating and worried that the sun had turned his neck red. He would request more sun cream, factor 50 at least. What time was it? It could be any time. He wasn't hungry.

Step away from the door.

Who is it? Hurriedly he put on his sandals. Damián? I asked you not to come today, Damián!

A middle-aged woman with red hair entered. The door was slammed shut fast, as if they'd just lobbed in a boa constrictor. She wore a white blouse, and her stockings enclosed the calves of a long-distance runner.

I went to all of your rallies and fundraising dinners, Doctor. I always voted for you.

The man snorted. They'd authorised him to receive visits from women and this was the first one they sent him?

Tell me, who sent you here and why?

No one's sent me. I'm here of my own accord. Each pore on her nose leaked, early morning dew, condensation from the very effort of existing. They told me you were selling pines and I've come to support you by buying one.

Who told you such a stupid thing? The line between laughter and rage threatened to dissolve. Please. They're for me. A hobby to pass the time, don't you see?

You were on TV yesterday, on the main news programme. There were some clips of you with those lovely plantpots of yours. All of us in the Party were inspired by this side of you we'd never seen before.

On the TV, you say? How long's that been going on? I didn't even know anyone had taken photos of me. I didn't authorise this.

Your lawyer said…

That idiot. I'll tell you the truth. He's lying and making me look like a foolish old man devoted to his garden to create an image of me that people aren't aware of, as you yourself have claimed. Please don't take this the wrong way, just go.

I won't. If you have a nursery, as I can see from here that you do, I don't understand why you won't sell me a pine. I can help you, that's why I came.

Come on, let me see you out, you're wasting your time. It was a euphemism, they were right outside the door. Had they sent her to intimidate him? Friends were enemies.

Let me speak with you a while. I've come from quite a way, my admiration for you is perfectly normal.

I don't doubt it. He thought: I'd feel more flattered if she were young. Everything's different now.

He knocked at the door to get rid of the awkward visitor; the redhead performed the unexpected, agile gesture of kneeling down without a word. From this angle she rolled down her right stocking and showed him her ankle. Dismayed, and with a detached curiosity, he approached her, stooping as he did so. A scar? How many women are tempted to try and seduce a man keloidically, take-pity-on-me, surviving, once-in-a-lifetime feat, I did it. He saw the tattoo. What on earth? But there was no doubt. It was his face on her ankle, the little cartoon from the flyers, his calling card.

The woman, mad as a hatter: You can touch it if you like – touch it. I've had it since you were elected.

Do you cover it up on purpose?

I cover it up because it's not for everyone. If someone can handle it, they can see it. It's a habit now.

Many thoughts galloped around his mind. He opened his mouth, about to give a speech from memory, and something else came out: My dear friend (his last wife hated him saying 'dear friend' to strangers; he couldn't help it), no matter what my lawyer tries to invent to get me out of here, no matter how much the Party smears half the world, or how fervently delusional women like yourself believe I am a saint – pause for breath – I deserve to be in here.

The woman stood. They were almost the same height. I know that you robbed people. She said it firmly.

I did a lot more than that. I robbed everyone.

I know.

Thank you for your visit. I am a simple gardener.

I'm a qualified lawyer.

Congratulations.

Do they feed you well?

Very well.

Do you have a kitchen?

No, I'm not allowed anything I could use to start a fire.

Do you not wear a watch?

The battery died.

Why pine trees?

Because they block unwanted views.

I understand. I hope everything gets better for you.

For you, too.

He hammered at the door to avoid shouting, Open up! like when his lawyer left.

Your pockets… They were talking to the woman now.

Returning to his concrete bench, he unclenched his jaw. He felt the desire to protect his home with serviceable devotion, no matter the cost; the silence, melody, a house where he would never lose his key, without stairs going down, or up, with a terrace, without any help.

He had, at last, almost everything he had ever wanted.

12.

SEVEN WAVES

My mother and I are going to see each other again today.

We're going to collect my father's life insurance money. Who said the dead don't do good deeds posthumously? She watches me come in, smiles. Stands up. A brief, adoring kiss. She used to introduce me: She's my best work and she's already flying away! I take in her red hair, fuchsia jumper, electric-blue trousers. As a girl, to be like her. Made-up, dressed to impress, ready to represent life. I should be happy to see her. I prepare myself. One chooses the places, most of the time. This situation chooses us. To be a photographer, comparing the shots taken of the same space year after year: 'I stood in the space that had framed the images to observe the changes and understand the angles.' I'm not fooling myself. Seven months, two and a half seasons have gone by: my mother is the same. Like this city: she adapts to everything.

When I'm nervous, I get the urge to urinate. I hold it in, I couldn't bear to hear her start to get agitated: It's not as if you've got a prostate!

She knows me.

We sign. Say thank you with mutilated words.
She says, shall we have lunch? My treat.

We choose the same dishes.
Are you going to give me half?
She pushes her plate towards me. A laugh half-open: You've already got your portion.
(I look at her. Her earrings tremble.)
He owed me 15,000 dollars. Why did he lend his brother the money I gave him?
They're both dead.
All day long making like an Egyptian, your father. One hand out the front, the other out the back.
He left me…
Show me one bit of paper that proves that.
He left me the same amount I spent.
Left you! Your father was always good at leaving.
You abandoned him.
I didn't come here to fight. If you've got your period, that's your problem. I'm in real pain.
What about my pain?
You're young. Young people don't feel pain, unless it's from too much living.
It was two weeks.
Be thankful, that's hardly any time.
What about you?
The ex-wife caring for the ex-husband? You think?
Remind me, when did you get divorced?
If you really want, I'll tell you what your father used to do to me. I swore I'd never talk about it. Now eat, and let me eat, too.
They were the longest two weeks ever.
It was never going to be a holiday. And children have a duty to take care of their parents. It's one of life's laws.
You've got money, you've always had it.

You get paid a salary every month, I don't!

(I take my chequebook from my jeans pocket. On his seventieth birthday, my father was at school teaching a class. The headmaster burst into the room and gave him a letter thanking him for his thirty years of service. His students squealed happily, quizzing him about his future, not understanding: the letter was a send-off. Forced optimism depressed my father. Until I take it to the bank to be cashed, this is just any old piece of paper.)

Don't shake it like that, come on, have a bit of respect. It's not just any old piece of paper.

(I fold the cheque in half, put it back in my pocket).

There's nothing I can do. If he didn't sign anything, that's it.

It's because of me that you know how it all happened.

(The waiter hovers near us holding a jug. He assesses our glasses, peering over uncertainly. Interrupting, confirming, huffing: a gadfly orchestra. Is everything OK? Shhh! we reply. The surprise at concurring. The man gives a little jump. Water falls on the floor and he gives us a startled look. He moves off, not noticing how the jug leaves a sad little trail behind it.)

When I say that I'm in real pain, I mean real pain, everything. Look at my poor hands.

Now why could that be.

I never laid a finger on you.

No, not one. Ten.

Never.

Selective memory, they call that.

You used to drive me crazy.

Are you admitting it at last?

I'm not admitting anything. What were we talking about?

Dad. It's because of me that you know how it all happened. I could have told you any old thing.

Don't look at me with that face or you know what's coming.

With those hands? I doubt it.

He's the one you should be annoyed with, not me. He refused to change his clothes, the same shirt day after day, all faded and dirty. Rags. What'll you do with his clothes? What'll you do with all of it?

Take it to the clinic, you said.

Who wants a dead man's clothes?

If someone dies in your house you never forget it.

I saved you from witnessing it. That furnace opening up, oh my God, I wish I could scrub that image from my mind. Your father on the bier with a smile like he was alive.

You want to scrub everything out.

It's curious, they give the mouth an expression that's real and fake at the same time. Like someone else's. A new expression. I don't know how to explain it. You finally understand what the phrase 'the sleep of the dead' means. They give you their shoes back. What for?

Shoes are important.

(My mother pushes back her chair and looks at her feet. I could say her name out loud: Teresa. Not Terry; she was never a Terry.)

One day you'll inherit all of mine. Whether they fit you – fit you properly – is another matter.

I don't fit into your clothes or your shoes.

We're not the same size and that's not my fault.

And what are we going to do with the ashes? Don't talk to me about scattering them in his favourite spots. A soul can't rest if it's spread about all over the place.

I don't know what to do with his ashes, Mum.

Bones stink. We can't smell them, but dogs can.

I was thinking about a boat.

They sit next to the urns waiting and waiting for their owners in vain. How's Mini?

On the open water, we could do it, one evening next summer.

No point being hypocrites. Your father was a world-class uprooter.

And if Mini doesn't get seasick.

The only people he cared about were, number one, himself; number two, himself; number three, you.

Mini won't move anymore. I talk to him, and nothing. Nothing at all.

He's more your dad's minion than ever.

Yup.

How're you getting on with Paolo?

I'm not.

You're not. What happened? I liked that kid.

Really?

He always smelled like he'd just got out of the shower.

I was mugged. I fought back and everything went to shit.

Why didn't you tell me?

I'm telling you now.

Were you hurt?

A bit, on my left leg. I was fighting this kid who was trying to grab my camera off me, he'd been following us. I tripped and he dragged me along for nearly half a block, but he didn't manage to get it.

Why didn't you hit him?

I don't know, he was practically a child; I couldn't do it.

And what did Paolo do, didn't he help you?

I was shouting, Paolo, Paolo! but he had a hat on and he couldn't see that there was another boy about to grab him. And zero visibility, with his sunglasses on.

What's wrong with defending yourself? I don't understand.

He said to me: You're in your own damn world. And if I hadn't defended myself, he would have said: Hey, he wasn't armed, you should have fucked him up.

Did you end it?

No, he did. But that's not what hurts the most.

It's not?

The sunglasses Dad gave me got broken.

Hang on – what sunglasses?

My birthday present.

How do you expect me to remember that if you spent it with him?

You didn't want to come.

That's what you think.

I went back to look for them. You could tell how bad the fight had been because of how the frames ended up.

The important thing is you're OK. It was just a pair of sunglasses. You can buy yourself a nicer pair.

I liked those sunglasses.

Are you still swimming?

I went back to it with a vengeance.

(My mother gets up. She grips my arms between her fingers.)

Of course – it shows! (She returns to her seat.) When you were a little girl, I didn't want to enrol you in swimming classes one bit. No one could get you out of the water. Then you started getting a man's back – such a tragedy.

I don't care if I have a man's back.

Meh, I wouldn't say it's a man's back or a woman's. It's neutral, it's just a back.

Nobody knows their own back.

And there'll always be someone who'll love you like that.

Like what?

With that back and those feet.

They're good for swimming.

You and water: a tidal wave.

You're the unpredictable one.

That's just my nature, no one can tame me.

Every seven waves you can be trusted.

And every seven waves I flip out. So what? That's what being in the swell is like, and swimmers would do well to get used to it.

In the sea everything is total uncertainty. That doesn't bother me at all. With you it's something else. We both know it's something else.

You and I are alike.

I don't think so.

One day, when I'm not here anymore, you'll admit that I taught you something.

(When she's not here anymore I'll sell the house, like a court-ordered public auction, 'take it or leave it,' with everything still inside, even our family photos. Perhaps the new inhabitants can put all the images together, debating and agreeing: 'The daughter has something of the mother about her.' 'They're not family, they don't look anything like each other.')

The gun.

You're not still harping on about that.

You aimed at me.

It wasn't real and you know it. Are you on a diet, is that why you're eating so slowly?

We didn't know that.

You were eight.

At that age guns and mothers are real.

I didn't aim it at you, don't exaggerate. And that's why your father hit me, or have you forgotten already?

He saw that you were pointing it at me – what could be worse for a father than seeing that?

He saw what he wanted to see. It was so hard for me to have you, everything with you was so hard that it pains me to hear you talk like this.

(The waiter has reappeared and is leaning against the wall observing us. His smooth face, dotted with little blemishes, looks like one of the restaurant's tablecloths. Is lunchtime over? I fulfil my task, I chew. Meat – was it always this tough? I can't swap the cutlery in my hands to cut it. I play for time.)

How can you distort a memory all this time?

Because I look hard at things, and I never grow tired of looking.

Well, look closely, then.

(I observe her. She holds my gaze. After a while she blinks and we both know she has lost. Whoever blinks first loses. If we were little girls it would be my turn, I would suggest the next game.)

What could you possibly remember? When you were seven you wrote me a darling little card. 'Thank you, Mum, for the peace in this house.'

I'd like to know what peace I was talking about.

You've always had a powerful imagination, ever since you were a girl. Go on, give it a go.

How do I know.

You adored me. I am a goddess to my daughter, I thought, she looks at me like no one else does, but how much longer will that look last?

(I look at her.) I guess it lasted as long as was necessary. (I look at her.)

I made bad decisions; I said yes to your father. I gave you everything. Even your blue eyes. Don't tell me that's not true. You have those eyes thanks to me.

As a child I thought that at some point I'd see everything in sky blue. Your eyes are grey.

You are how you are because of me. Sooner or later you'll accept it. But we both know where that chronic tight-fistedness comes from. It comes from the same place your feet do.

So I look like him – so what?

All that's left is for you to stop washing.

You can be a real bitch sometimes.

That doesn't surprise me, I'm your mother.

An indisputable fact.

Waiter! Waiter! Excuse me! (From the wall the man's eyebrows make an appearance. He raises them. My mother scribbles in the air with an imaginary pen.)

Do you remember? When I used to ride in your car and Dad would drive his in front of us, lead the way, you'd say, you never learned the route yourself.

I'm terrible at map-reading but even so, no one can say I ever got lost, no one!

I used to wonder, when will they drop? Dad's fag ends would whizz past and land on the tarmac. I'd count them; they measured the way back home.

What about me? I smoked too.

You smoked too. But if I ever turned around looking for a trace of you, the little red lights had already disappeared from the road.

I am a *mother.*

Something that apparently…

You will never be! I've gone above and beyond my duty in life. I deserve your respect, everyone's respect. What do you want from me?

I want you to ask me, just once. Just once. How do I feel about Dad's death.

That's it.

I don't know why I get my hopes up with you.

Because in your stupid head, doing something over and over equals happiness. Waaaaaaiter!

I don't want to change anything. I might even feel grateful. Living's the heroic thing. But you...

I did what I could. What goes around comes around, eventually. And if you expect me to ask for forgiveness,

I have no reason to. You corner me so you can force me to do it.

You didn't respect Dad's wishes.

(My closest friends insist: There must be *something* nice about her! It's so difficult to connect one's mother with something that saves and kills. She studied cookery; the house was a restaurant open twenty-four hours a day. It was so wonderful when she was distracted from us, devoted to something else. She gave me a set of recipes she had written down in an exercise book. The front page had a space to write the teacher's name and she wrote: Your mum. My mother, funny, generous. Her irresistible ambiguity. A doctor, the greengrocer, people passing through: She's so lovely. She says hello, thank you. You're so lucky to have her. I, amazed at the other version, viable, perishable.)

Sometimes I think you're playing games with me and I take every game very seriously.

I'm going away, Mum. I'm telling you in plenty of time so I can leave Mini with you.

A dog in my house? No! No siree! Where are you going? Where is that idiot waiter? He's pretending he can't hear us!

I don't know yet.

Can I come with you?

No.

And to think I came here to talk to you about your father's car.

I gave it to him.

Where's that written down? I knew it! I knew money was the reason you were acting so aloof. I need to save for my old age. Who knows what future awaits me all on my own!

Your old age is now. This is your old age.

Good God, but you're cruel. What would your father say?

I don't know.

I would say that he saw you and that was it. He never saw me.

I would say that he saw you and he saw the gun. And that was it.

You're the spitting image of each other. A photocopy. Peas in a pod.

And you love me just as I am.

I've always loved you. It would kill me to think you didn't know that. Grow up for once, for the love of God.

I help her into a taxi.

The driver says: Careful, it's raining and everything's wet, put your head in slowly, if there's one thing we've still got it's time.

My mother to the driver: Take me to the bank four blocks from here.

I don't drive. I never learned. I do everything on foot. I'll let my mother have the car if she wants it that much.

Before she shuts the door, her voice: Let's not wait another seven months before seeing each other, you're all I've got left.

She smiles at me. I take refuge in her smile and for a moment I think: she's not asking for anything in return, she hasn't taken anything from me.

I'll go for a walk. The squares on the pavement are still soaking wet and slippery. I have loved her so much. The first thing I'll forget is her voice. My head hurts. I'd like a hug from my mother right now. It's rare that it rains here, the afternoon an almost nocturnal grey, the red lights of the antennae have started to pulse. It's the first time I notice it. In the park: footballs, blankets, dogs, mothers, bikes, pigeons, murmurs, movements. Statues of nameless heroes, on horses with their terrible hooves in the air. It smells of morning, of freshly drenched grass.

It's still raining beneath those trees, the wind heaves and shakes them. Thick drops fall onto clothes with an unfamiliar power. A few children shout in amazement and jump and laugh. Others cannot stand it and ask to go back home.

TRANSLATOR'S NOTE

In one of the stories in Katya Adaui's *Here Be Icebergs*, 'Where the Hunts Take Place', a seemingly secure family house is besieged by an unknown, malevolent intruder who daubs the outside walls with squashed fruit, destroys carefully cultivated plants, and unsettles everything. Scientists are called in to investigate and, as one of them observes the odd behaviours of the family who lives there, he comments: 'Families are a Lazarus taxon, they never go extinct'. In palaeontology, a Lazarus taxon is one that disappears for one or more periods from the fossil record, only to re-appear again later. In conservation biology and ecology, it can refer to species or populations that were thought to be extinct but are then rediscovered. The term refers to the story in the Gospel of John, in which Christ raises Lazarus from the dead, and the phrase might serve as an alternative epigraph to this collection of lyrical, hard-to-categorise short stories. Families are the constellations around which the book circles, their Lazarus-like pull at once devastating yet irresistible.

The dysfunction in the families who feature here ranges from the relatively unremarkable – (two sisters' starkly different experiences of childhood) to the traumatic (a boy being abused by his cousin in a basement), but connecting them all is the constant push and pull that forces families apart, sometimes to the point of rupture, and yet frequently brings each member back into orbit with the others, no matter how difficult or self-destructive this might feel. In the story, 'The Colour of Ice,' the narrator speaks of her mother's 'favourite painting: *The Destruction of Pompeii* […] From the reflection of the light on the water, the calm hours of the sea, I used to think it was a lost kingdom, Atlantis or something similar. I only saw the destruction when I found out what the title was.' Given the psychological violence we witness caregivers perpetrating throughout the collection, the observation on John Martin's vivid painting seems to allude obliquely to how we often fail to recognise the brutality of families when observing them from the outside – or even at times from the inside. Inevitably, in any tale concerning families, Tolstoy's famous line comes to mind, but as well as examining how 'each unhappy family is unhappy in its own way,' Adaui's book also reminds us that being able to see exactly how – or whether – some families are unhappy involves fearless looking, on the part of family members or, in this case, on the part of the writer herself.

This looking, this necessary observation, is something children in dysfunctional families often learn to do. The narrator of 'The Hunger Angel' finds a way to take a step back from the action when things becomes too painful: her parents 'hit each other. I step between them. He picks me up off the floor and she slaps at me in the air. […] It's crystal clear to me: I am not what unites them […] I am not them. I write and I save myself. It happens to me, but I manage to be The Spectator.' This stepping back in order to spectate is also a vital skill for a writer – a survival tactic turned valuable professional attribute. The child observing parental discord becomes hyper aware (the state of any writer!) to all fluctuations in mood, in atmosphere. 'I write and I save myself'. An intense, life-saving focus on someone in a family – from a careful distance – is what marks nearly all the stories in this collection, a focus that urges us to reflect on what it means to create a narrative for oneself (both within and outside one's family of origin) as a means of self-preservation and also of creativity. We witness the young girl in the first story learning how to create effect (how to invent a narrative about herself) when she is asked to read by a priest: 'I modulate my voice to create a special effect, at least among the believers in the first few rows. When I return to my pew, a few old ladies smile at me as if at a favourite granddaughter. I think: if someone comes in with a machine gun right now, I will leap in front of the priest and die for him so that everyone says: That girl is a saint.' This conscious manipulation of how she is perceived, this ability to imagine how certain actions she might perform will affect how others read her, is her learning how to be a writer.

The initial pull for me of Katya's book was the chance to return, through translation, to Lima, to Peru. Working on it during lockdown was, in a way, like time-travelling (I haven't been back there since the early 2000s when I was a student), but also just like travelling – unable to go anywhere, like most of us, I did feel in a way that I had returned to the country where I fell in love with Spanish, with Latin America, with moving between two languages and thinking about what that means in terms of identity and personhood. The sights, sounds, smells of the city where I spent my year abroad came back to me as I read – Lima, where many of the stories occur, was the first place I fully grasped what it means to live in another language: to think in it and dream in it and to feel, when one goes back to English, briefly, that one has stepped over to the other side and is looking back at one's homeland (homelanguage?) in astonishment.

Neither Lima nor Peru feature particularly explicitly in the book, but there are occasional unmistakeable images that appear: we see 'metal-framed bulls laden with fireworks [...] bouncing off roofs, pointing with their horns, with the whole of their sinewy bodies, skeleton and bulk, until finally charging with their pointed, smoking heads'; the characters in 'The Colour of Ice' drive past 'walls on either side of the highway [...] painted with the slogans of mayoral hopefuls;' and there is one brief mention of the fear-laden days of the Shining Path: 'The terrorists [who] blow up electricity pylons.' Each time these images crop up, I was transported, as I read and translated, back to that dusty, noisy, surprising, grey, friendly, contradictory city in brief flashes. When I returned from Lima after a year of living there, the city followed me home to England, and I would hear, purely in my mind, the sounds of fruit sellers hawking their wares from metal and wooden carts, of the elaborate sing-song horns the drivers of the small inner-city buses known as micros would install in their vehicles, of the screech of lime-green parakeets. Lima had imprinted itself onto my brain, and these sensory hallucinations came to me as I walked around the streets of Bristol, and they came back to me once more as I moved deeper into Katya's book.

These brief, unbidden flashes are also how memory comes back to us. The stories in *Here Be Icebergs* range from more traditional-looking constructions with a beginning, a middle and an end, displaying some sort of progression, to ones whose structure has been upset or upended. Adaui has said that she tries to write in the same way that memory comes, and the story where this approach is clearest is the first one, a series of 68 short, numbered sections appearing in descending order, which gradually reveal the narrator's experience of several family relationships, just as a cracked mirror on the floor slowly reveals to us our own face: unexpectedly, fragmentarily, jarringly. The numbered fragments appear as memories appear to us, not in a linear order but rather bubbling up randomly, or triggered by a sound or a smell or a piece of music. The disjointed order here mirrors the disjointed nature of the girl's upbringing and the care she is given, a mother who gives her presents and then takes them away, whose love is patchy and conditional, withheld when she feels this is necessary, a father who is not fully present due to unmanaged grief and who blames his own children for his inability to leave their mother. Often the sentences in this first story are jagged, unmediated bursts of memory, unmediated by analysis or linking sentences. 'My first memory. Two years old. Nappy down around my knees. Hand. Cot. I scream. Nobody. I slip. Face. They run.' All the stories here, though, are interested in how language is imperfect, with fragments often appearing joltingly on the page in the same way that difficult memories from childhood can irrupt into our consciousness, or into our seemingly 'perfect' families. Just as a pun or swearword, arising almost unbidden into speech, unsettles (and the book is also interested in this kind of wordplay), so an undesirable memory from childhood can arise and destabilise our families, our relationships and our own selves. In translation it was important not to try and tidy up these seemingly unfinished fragments – their jagged nature is key to the jagged way memory works. In making some of the difficult decisions about what to do with, for instance, the many times when a potentially ambiguous infinitive is used in the Spanish, I am indebted to the wise suggestions of my editor, Robin Myers. Her poet's sensibility helped the translation to retain some of the lyrical aspects of Katya's prose.

As much as Katya's book is concerned with using language as a tool to reflect the nature of memory and experience, it is also interested in the imperfection of language as a system. Like memory, language is incomplete, imperfect, and can sometimes do harm. In 'This is the Man', the narrator describes what his cousin Sandro does during the abuse he carried out. 'He'd put his arms around me. He'd talk a lot, saying any old thing that came into his head. I heard only a tangle of words, I didn't want to listen; if I understood I would always understand, and I didn't want to.' The narrator recognises here that words can only do so much, and can sometimes do too much. He turns to painting, a non-verbal activity, as an escape, as a way of re-configuring what happened to him: 'Adulthood is an artificial beach the mind prolongs. This is why, when I paint Sandro, I paint him as a child, at the same age. If I were to paint him as an adult, I would hate him.' Similarly, the narrator of 'The Colour of Ice' finds himself unable to speak – 'My lips moved without articulating anything. As if I'd forgotten language and its effects' – when his companions commit a shocking (unspeakable?) act of violence during a road trip to Ticlio, high up in the Andes, supposedly the highest railway junction in the world. When they get there, they realise this claim to fame is obsolete, a junction in China having surpassed Ticlio in altitude, and yet 'the sign continued to lie and [the tourists] believed it, words sustained by words.' Along with others in the collection, this story asks what use words are in such situations, when a brutal reality has taken effect making language seem impotent, as after a senseless murder, or when a truth has overtaken seemingly timeless printed words on a sign. Just as the book moves between examining how families are destructive and yet compelling, so it moves between asking how much language can ever really do and enacting the fact that it is all we have to describe, imperfectly and yet often beautifully, our own complicated realities. Such an examination is music to any translator's ears, accustomed as we are to moving between frustration at the 'impossible' nature of our task and joy when we find a solution that sings in a new and unexpected voice.

Here Be Icebergs takes a fearless look at difficult families, at ruptures, and yet each story is also about a reaching-out across seemingly uncrossable divides, an attempt to make contact despite the ruptures (as any psychotherapist will tell you, it is not a rupture that is problematic in a relationship, it is how this rupture is repaired). The ex-presidential candidate in 'Gardening' is behind bars, has regrets about how he treated his children, and yet a woman comes to visit him and to express her support. The family in 'Where the Hunts Take Place' are trapped in their house, and yet each family member is attempting in their own way to solve the mystery. Mrs Queta has a door shut in her face by a much-admired neighbour in 'Lovebird', and yet experiences a long-forgotten sense of freedom as she releases her unwanted present of a lovebird into the depths of the sky. There is, throughout, a bridging of the unbreachable space between us, and a sense of hope as Adaui examines the way we ceaselessly attempt contact despite all the evidence that each of us is an unknowable island.

Rosalind Harvey
Coventry, November 2021

Director & Editor: Carolina Orloff
Director: Samuel McDowell

www.charcopress.com

Here Be Icebergs was published on
80gsm Munken Premium Cream paper.

The text was designed using Bembo 11.5 and ITC Galliard.

Printed in February 2022 by TJ Books
Padstow, Cornwall, PL28 8RW using responsibly
sourced paper and environmentally-friendly adhesive.